ELEGANT THREAT

ON THE DEMISE OF CAPTAIN FANTOMAS PATTON-GUERRERO AND LOSS OF LA AMENAZA ELEGENTE

BRANDON H. BELL

For Lauri.
And for Bethany, Sheridan,
Jordan, Chelsea, and Delany.
You are all "slicks" to me.

Foreword

I have been telling readers about Brandon H. Bell since I first read his work in the slush-pile the first month I was producing *M-Brane SF* magazine. In the slightly more than two years since *M-Brane SF #1*, I have published Brandon's stories twice more in the magazine and in a couple of anthologies (*Things We Are Not* and the *M-Brane SF Quarterly #1*), and I have been gratified to see, as his list of publishing credits steadily lengthens, that other editors are seeing what I see in this extraordinarily imaginative and intellectual writer.

The story you are about to read is a marvel, and the realization in print of a project that Brandon Bell has been working on for a long time. He has created a rich, lavish, fascinating and sometimes frightening Post-Singularity interplanetary milieu. Some lucky readers have had a chance to peer into it a couple of times already: one of his first published short stories, "Best Gift" (*Return to Luna*, Hadley Rille 2008) was, as Bell describes it on his website, "a tale about Sterling Suits, Neo-Dromedaries, and the persistence of love, trust, and faith on the lunar surface." The next glimpse into this strange world was in *M-Brane SF #5* (June 2009), with the story "Abraham Discovers an Artifact Impenetrable to All Harm," an enigmatic and startling story about an unusual family struggling to make their way in the universe at the edges of an impending war between humans and Post-humans. These stories were so fascinating that my only complaints were that they

were too short and that there weren't enough of them. But now, with *Elegant Threat*, we finally get to spend a longer time in Bell's world.

Elegant Threat—the story of people who wrangle aquatic fauna from the harrowing tides of the moon Shanama against a backdrop of imminent conflict with the mysterious Post-humans and sectarian strife within their own ranks—was envisioned by its author as the first of a triptych of stories that will eventually comprise a much longer novel. But this story herein—a novella of about thirty thousand words—is also complete, self-contained and will satisfy readers even if the other portions are never seen (though all readers of this one will certainly clamor for the rest and Bell likely shall feel obliged to produce it soon enough).

Bell has deployed an interesting and unexpected literary device in telling this story. Its subtitle, *On the Demise of Captain Fantomas Patton-Guerrero and Loss of La Amenaza Elegente*, gives the reader a big clue up front essentially how the story is going to end, as does the very first chapter's final line: "...*La Amenaza Elegente* dropped toward the planet, beginning its descent toward the place that would soon become its grave." As with an ancient Greek tragic play or a Shakespeare drama, we go into it knowing that Captain Fantomas and his ship are doomed but the fascination lies in seeing how and why this disaster unfolds. And even though the ending is foretold from the earliest pages, the reader will not see coming the stunning sequence of events that bring about that ending. This way of telling the story, as if it is a recounting of an event that the reader may have heard of before, adds an alluring patina of history to it. But what really makes this story and this way of telling it succeed is the way that Bell draws such lovely, nuanced characters and makes the reader really care about them enough to hope that maybe somehow, against all odds, they will still avert tragedy even though we already know that the *Amenaza* is not going home again.

Now, without further delay, please visit spectacular, deadly Shanama and witness the fate of *La Amenaza Elegente*.

—Christopher Fletcher, Editor, *M-Brane SF*

1
Above Shanama

There were seven Spanish Angels,
At the alter of the Sun.
They were prayin' for the lovers,
In the valley of the gun.
When the battle stopped,
And the smoke cleared.
There was thunder from the throne.
And seven Spanish angels,
Took another angel home.

—Troy Seals & Eddie Setser,
"Seven Spanish Angels"
(The song could be heard from the main bay after the slicks set to work prior to drop one, and plays during the opening scene of Professor Patton's documentary about these events.)

Pristina stood on the ship's bridge with her daughters and stared upon the roiling waters obscuring the face of Shanama. Cancer, sixteen standard, and Toro, eight, shifted in disinterest and unease respectively. The first mate's boy pretended not to watch them from his post.

She rubbed the lobe of Toro's ear and the girl leaned into her mother. They'd been up getting ready for several hours past bedtime. Toro's eyes were puffy and both girls had grown weary of each other. Cancer huffed and sighed with clock-like regularity, shifting from hip to hip in boredom.

"Wish I was back at Salem," Cancer whispered to herself. Pristina pretended not to hear, further frustrating her daughter.

View ports lined the starboard, port, and forward bulkheads of the bridge, the last in a single vast pane The captain's chair dominated the room with additional stations situated along the expanse of the forward view. A sound-powered phone hung on the rear wall beside a small kitchenette with sink, pantry, and coffee pot. The hatch into the bridge gaped on the floor behind them, the ladder leading down into the central access corridor.

"Momma, we're landing in *that?*" Toro asked. She had dark hair and eyes and was easy to smile, much like her father, but also moody and given to reading more than might be healthy. She had a slight bulge to her belly and baby fat in her cheeks.

"No, mi ha, of course not. Look out the ports behind us. What do you see?" Pristina smiled down at the girl who already wore brass goggles upon her forehead in imitation of her father, the great Captain Fantomas Patton-Guerrero. Hers were shiny-new where the brass on her father's was blemished green. A small injustice she weathered stoically.

"Ferdowsi," Toro said, the striated clouds of

the huge planet reflecting in her eyes and goggle lenses. Blue across most of its face with white clouds about the polar regions.

"Use the proper name, mi ha. You'll be apprenticed to Khalid Sujjad and while he will not care, some of the slicks he employs will." In respect for slick customs she'd be cutting her own hair down to mere stubble. And in compensation for her husband, who would not.

"Who cares what they think?" Cancer muttered. Pristina slapped the back of her head hard enough to signal it wasn't totally in jest.

"Shah Ferdowsi, I see, Momma," Toro said, bunching her face in a dour glance at her sister.

"Yes. The waters on Shah Ferdowsi's moon, Shanama, are tied gravitationally to the gas giant. Note, the moon itself is not tidally locked; it rotates just like Oasis."

"I don't understand," Toro said.

"Because you're stupid," Cancer suggested, getting hit from both sides. She, too, had new goggles that were nowhere to be seen and likely lost. Pristina sighed and thought this a good idea after all. The child grew older and had little appreciation for the accoutrements of her life and less drive to contribute in any way. Khalid would push her to and beyond her limits during the internship. Pristina smiled at her oldest daughter, but felt sad. She would not be a child much longer.

"Toro, in about fifteen hours we'll still be above the same spot on Shanama, but we'll have rotated along with that spot. The land below will only have a foot or so of water."

Toro nodded and gazed out at the waters of the moon. She did not understand but she would.

As they stepped from the bridge Pristina smiled at the boy and placed her hand on his wrist. She could tell Cancer had taken his heart already, and she was oblivious.

"You're doing a fine job, mi ho. Amr."

The boy beamed.

After seeing the girls to bed she thought to remind Fantomas to get some sleep himself. Down the central access, out of family country and into the common galley, then past various work sheds, Pristina padded. The briny sting of seawater and the kelpie musk permeated the air in the brightly lit, watery main hold, where she lingered a moment. She wanted to avoid the foreman during this busy time, if possible. She descended to hold level and started forward again until she came to the portal from which her husband's baritone wafted.

"So she tells me 'I will call it *Hearts of Darkness,*' this satisfied look in her eyes," Fantomas laughed. He carries well the extra pounds from his drinking and his smile flashed often though he was, basically, a serious man. His hair, even now in the oily environment of the slick vessel, fanned out from his scalp in a frizzy explosion, gray blooms at his temples and peppering his beard and mustache. Worry lines creased his forehead and he drifted in conversations. He lost the beat of those interactions and sometimes spoke out of turn, or offered silence in place of comment. He could be dull enough to weather any man's offense, and sharp enough to cut such a man to his knees, if required.

He preferred to wear a lazy smile and enjoy a stiff drink with friends or slicks working honest and hard in his charge.

"You should not mock your wife, so. She is a good woman," Khalid grinned despite himself. One of the fem slicks had set up shop as the resident barber —earning some extra credits during the transfer orbit into Ferdowsi space— ,and he was still getting used to the braids the young woman had talked him into. Excess hair in a slick ship became an encumbrance amid all the Kelpie oil. Already his skin sheened with a thin film and he could taste it in his throat.

Fantomas guffawed so hard he struggled to speak and put a hand on Khalid's knee to steady himself and draw the other man's attention. The gesture signaled the familiarity of their friendship amid the rigid mores of slick society. *The Final Bushido*, Fantomas often joked.

"'You know your Earth media', I told her," Fantomas breathed in a quick slur of disbelief.

"I do not understand, Fantomas." Khalid raised his eyebrows and cocked his head, looking back to the unifoil he'd been repairing. They labored in the forward equipment bay where they could have some time away from the slicks.

"Bah," Fantomas said with a wave of his hand, growing somber. "A joke explained is a poor thing indeed." He perched in the saddle of one of the unifoils and revved its engine, then turned it off, satisfied at the electric whine.

"Indeed," Khalid said.

"I'm glad I am so good at amusing you, my husband," Pristina said, stepping into the chamber. She allowed a faint, familiar smile to touch her lips.

The men stared at her in surprise and she smirked and shook her head.

"Foolish boys, both," she mocked. "The girls are to bed. I thought to suggest you do the same soon. I'd like to see you before operations start." She raised an eyebrow.

The two men laughed and continued their inspection and maintenance of the unifoils. Khalid noticed Fantomas had not yet cut his hair.

"The girl, Boski, is still doing haircuts," he said.

"I'm not shaving. Just keeping it tied up."

"We'll see how that works out," Khalid said.

"Yes we will," Pristina said.

"Will you be shaving, mistress?" Khalid asked.

Nodding, she said, "I'll make a visit to this Boski before retiring."

Khalid bowed his head in approval.

"Next we check on the kelpies, yes?" Fantomas said, standing.

"Of course, my captain," Khalid replied.

"To bed then, my silly man," Pristina said though she held little hope he would comply.

Nilay saluted Pristina, the captain's wife, as she passed him on the stairs.

"Foreman," she said. She sported goggles, wet suit, and sheathed blades. A slick herself.

He wondered at her hair but turned back to the rabble in his charge.

"Come on, we got hours left! That won't do for atmo, son," Nilay shook his head and walked up the ladder to the upper deck and the water bottle he'd left there. The oils infused and coated his skin, eyes, throat. He swallowed instead of coughing, maintaining his command demeanor.

A score and ten slicks toiled in the main bay, preparing for the first drop. Nilay surveyed the group. A half-dozen were known to him from past tours. Slicks aged fast and either retired after a wise management of their funds, or found themselves struggling for a place in the labor pools back at Dar al-Salam. Or worse, Rub al-Ghali.

Slicks descended onto Nama to wrangle kelpies and other of the native fauna to ship back to Salem and Golly, the colonies on the only other habitable planet in the system, Oasis. Fauna and flora on Oasis was truly alien, whereas Nama's, while unfamiliar to the first ships that arrived in-system a century past, was based on DNA. Rigel Kent's great mystery. The ship mistress fancied herself a scientist and talked at length about 'the implications.' Nilay respected the woman. Sensible with her children and devoted to her husband. But on the one occasion they spoke he could think of nothing to say in response except, *it implies we have something proper to eat.* She'd demurred conversation with him afterward.

"Hey. Hey! You. All You. Stop and listen up," his voice, low and graveled from a run-in with a tape shark that had almost ripped his throat open, drew the slick's attention. Most already wore goggles on foreheads, gloves, stockings, wet suits/shorts, and a few held a kelpie beside them, petting, mewing to, and feeding the beasts. *Good.*

"You've got down time until the clock hits Hour One," Nilay gestured at the chronometer above him. "Assemble back here at that time and be ready for work. Crew leaders," the tension thickened among the slicks. Leaders could expect a larger commission than the others. "Waseem, Nirav, Evar, Boski, and Gustavo. Divide up now and everyone know who your lead is. I'll see you here at time." And with that Nilay took his water bottle and went forward to report his decisions, uninterested in the grumbling that would follow. Everyone thought they should be a lead. They always did.

Amr loved Cancer. He hoped soon to speak with her, but what to say, he had not yet decided.

He stood watch on the bridge, awaiting the Captain and his father's return. Cancer, Toro, and their mother had entered the bridge and distracted him with their banter for a time, but they too had left him alone. The girl's mother was a kind and beautiful woman who made a point of speaking with the slicks and counted his father, she once told him, as a close friend not just to the Captain but to her as well.

Amr, tall and lanky at fifteen, ready for another growth spurt that might render him taller even than his father, held so much energy in his meager chest and limbs that he constantly fidgeted and adjusted, cleared his throat, and scratched at the skin below the goggles. He still needed a shave from the slick, Boski: she, too, was pretty after a fashion. The hard and lean, mean as hell if she needed to be, kind of way. Amr, who still worked at his studies toward a generalist degree so that he might then study at University in Dar al-Salam, knew his preoccupation with females to be hormonal.

Cancer was beautiful. They had not seen each other since the previous year and she had *grown*. But she had also grown hard, in a way much different than Boski, who was kind in her own gruff manner.

"Daydreaming, son?" the Captain sprang from the ladder leading into the bridge followed by Khalid, Amr's father.

"No, sir! High tide is below us," Amr gestured out the port.

"Take a gander, then. The water you'll see will be knee-deep," the big man settled into the Captain's Chair while Khalid poured two cups of coffee.

"May I have a cup, too, father?"

The men glanced at each other and Amr thought he saw a smile pass between them. They were tricky sometimes, more like brothers than first mate and skipper. Amr readied himself for some obscure test of his wits. The Captain treated Amr like a nephew and often presented him as his 'God son,' though the man professed to disbelief and none of the Shaivist or even the Sunnis back on Dar al-Salam understood the title's implications.

His father pulled a third ceramic cup from a

small pantry and poured a measure into it.

Amr drank his coffee black without protest or comment. The three stared out toward the bulges of water below: bands of water piling up under the intense and convoluted gravity acting on the moon. *Imagine a sine wave* the Captain said when Amr asked about the odd bands. *Increasing in the middle and decreasing to either side. You have the big bulge in the middle, troughs between it and the first of the mid bulge pairs. The same across the second set of mid bulges and the two pairs of little bulges on down to the mere high tide, where the water falls from the sine wave.*

Amr's eyes unfocused, when the railing behind him twanged with weight.

Nilay, the slick foreman, swung up from the ladder and onto the bridge.

"Captain, gentlemen," he nodded at Amr and Khalid then turned back to Fantomas. Nilay's voice was deep, his face swarthy and bland, and the man's neck had a chewed look to it. *There are dangers on Shanama even in low tide*, his father had told him, but no more. And Nilay didn't do small talk.

"Thought I'd let you know before I get some shut-eye. Leads are Boski, Evar, Gustavo, Nirav, Waseem."

"How do you feel?" the Captain asked him. Amr didn't understand the question, but Nilay answered without pause.

"The two women will do fine: they're tough. I know Nirav: he's young but sharp. Waseem and Gustavo are new to me."

"What made you choose them?" Khalid asked.

"Waseem is devout. Very put together. A little

distant from the others but already has a kelpie and his equipment in good order. Several of the others are his cousins so his crew will be easy for him to lead. Gustavo is everyone's friend: life of the party. We'll see if he can pull off the lead position." Nilay paused, a sour look on his face.

"Yes, Nilay?" The Captain asked.

"I don't like how green this bunch is. Is the apprenticeship wise?"

Amr's eyebrows knit together. What did he care about the Captain's daughter apprenticed to the first mate and Captain?

"Amr!" the Captain bellowed, squeezing oil from his beard and whiskers in a thought-filled gesture.

"Captain!" Amr stood straight, coffee cup held in front of him, ignoring the hot liquid draining down his tunic.

"Do you think you can shadow Nilay without getting in his way?"

Nilay turned to Amr with a dark gaze. He maintained a thin growth of hair across his scalp, trimmed precisely, and no facial hair. His eyes stared, set wide in his dark face and full of disinterest. Goggles hung around his chewed neck.

"What? I mean, yes, Captain. Yes, I can," Amr looked from man to man, realization dawning.

"I get to be a slick," Amr whispered.

"You'll go to University on Dar al-Salam," his father and the Captain said in unison.

"But I suppose in the meantime we'll see that you know how to be a man. So when you walk the hallowed halls you can stand up to all those dry civies," Nilay said. "Good day, gents. See you at

Hour One. I'm hitting the bunk. Muster in the bay at that time, Amr. Introduce yourself to the leads and let them know you are at their beck and call."

"Yes. Yes sir!" Amr said, but the foreman had already slid down the ladder and was gone.

Scant hours before wake-up and Hour One, Fantomas made his way by the girl's room and peeked in on them. Family country sprawled just rear of the bridge and forward of the community mess. Cancer lay folded into an embryonic bundle on her bunk and even in sleep looked angry. Fantomas recalled times when she and he were buddies, but that time had passed. Toro lay stretched out, arms up, legs splayed, blankets kicked to the floor. Goggles still on her forehead. He grinned and shook his head.

Fantomas walked over to her bunk, covered her, pulled the goggles off her forehead, and hung them from the bedpost. Drawings studded the bulkhead and Toro's violin case lay beside her on the bed like a doll.

She still loved him, at least. He kept trying with her big sister, but his hope waned with each passing day.

He left the room and headed to Pristina and a few hours sleep before droptime.

Toro, sleeping, reached for her violin case and pulled it close. In her dream she rode a narwhal of old earth, eviscerating ghost sharks and mermen while her father beamed and the slick crew hollered in excitement.

Her imaginings tended toward exoticism, the

stuff of fairy tale books and thus old earth fauna and Sterling-suited black figures, the Post-human scourge of sol system. Cancer made fun of her pretend games and impromptu violin performances in the halls of the ship when she would tame or enchant a tiger, earthman, or daliphant with the music. Cancer remained beyond her power and mocked her.

In the dream even the dark silhouettes of Earths stood in the water, watching her and the narwhal stare down a megalodon, the narwhal waving its unicorn horn jeeringly while she stood upon its back and played a melancholy tune mounting into a tremulo that frightened the ship-sized shark and drove it back into the receding bulge of water.

Afterward, in the dream, they feasted on cakes and sweetmeats and sang songs while she played her strings.

In the dream even Cancer smiled.

For a time, silence spread through the ship punctuated by honks and whines from kelpies in the main hold. That silence settled in and ruled even among the kelpie mounts, until personal alarms blared here and there throughout the vessel. Men and woman began to stir. Sounds of labor returned. Hour One approached.

Amr knew *La Amenaza Elegente* better than anyone. The bridge lay forward and topmost but for the escape pod. Just aft and below that lay family country including Amr and his father's quarters, then the community mess. The foreman's quarters and office came next, big window overlooking the main bay. Stay at quarters level, and the walkways aft led to guest country, where the slicks bunked. His father told Amr this was a rarity among slick captains: treating the slicks as guests with assigned living areas and some measure of privacy. Many slick captains treated their slicks worse than the chattel they wrangled. Here one of the many reasons men like Khalid and Nilay stayed on with the Captain.

If one descended the ladder beside the foreman's overlooking office and then turned back and headed forward, one's feet remained dry and there lay various equipment bays, engineering and environmental, a medical facility, and fire-station one.

Amr had no business in those dry, safe forward areas. He paused on the final half-flight of stairs dropping into the oily, tepid waters of the main hold. Long and wide as the sports stadium in Dar al-Salam, though the upper deck acted as an oppressive ceiling for all but this central open area criss-crossed by the walkways above. Bright LED arrays lit the space with a fake glow and a cacophony filled the air: water lapping at bulkheads, kelpies nawing and whining, men and women calling sharp orders and grunted replies. Someone opened up a unifoil and traversed the space to the main bay door. There he racked the 'foil beside the door and whistled with fingers pressed to his mouth. One of the kelpies surged toward him, raising up out of the water and standing almost vertical on its articulated tail. The man rode back on the beast's saddle and jumped down to the metal beachhead just behind Amr and grabbed another 'foil.

Skin crawling, Amr realized one of the slick woman stared at him from the restless water below where a dazzle of kelpies were confined in a small corral. She cocked her head at him and gestured.

Get your ass over here, he imagined her saying.

He plunked from the stairs into the knee-deep water and waded over to Boski. The water smelled of fish, salt, seaweed, with hints of sweat and kelpie oil. The oil shimmered on the surface like sullen rainbows. Boski, one of the crew leaders and the woman he had kept from sleep too few hours earlier in search of a hair cut. She had not, like most of the slicks, shaved her own head clean, but instead sported short, tight braids.

"Are you stupid? You don't let slicks see you stand around, gawking. You work. You work harder than anyone. You muster first, you leave last. You help when it's reasonable, but you don't *need* anyone's help. You don't take flak, but you never, ever take offense. Maybe, if you have better ears than a brain and you listen to what I am saying to you, you'll live through this."

Her accent reminded him of the Shaivists back home and he smiled, trying to see her eyes through the reflections in her goggled. She shook her head in response and he stopped smiling.

"Yes, ma'am. What can I do?"

Apparently he'd be fodder for the crew leaders until Nilay had time for him. He thought it'd be fun to move the unifoils forward, feed the kelpies, or something like that. Instead Boski led him onto the dry deck, over to the equipment lockers, and demonstrated the proper method for prepping and stowing packs into each locker.

"If someone gets hurt because you slacked off, young man, it's me you will deal with. Yes?"

"Amr," he said.

The woman stopped, mouth tight. She wrenched her goggles down around her neck and thrust her face so close to his that he started, both afraid and thrilled at her proximity. Her breath stank of meat.

"Slicks use your name when they respect you. Do you think anyone else down in that water is going to be so kind as to call you 'young man?'"

"Probably not," he said.

"Probably not," she agreed.

He turned back to the packs.

"Put your goggles on. When you hear the foreman, find me," she said, leaving him to his work.

Hour One. Cancer stalked from family country back toward the platform over-looking the main hold, brown eyes leveled and ready. The whole ship stank like the damn kelpies and oil covered everything including the dirty slicks and her family. The bleating beasts and their wrangler's hollers and whoops echoed in the hall along with the undertone of splashing water. The main shaft lights had been dimmed for descent and as she neared the hold, the light grew blinding. Cancer's skin remained as dry as she could maintain and she wore none of the slick gear Fantomas had given her with his big stupid smile.

She hated him.

She didn't understand why her mom couldn't be alone. She was weak, Cancer had long ago decided, weakness the one unforgivable sin in Cancer's morality. That, and disagreeing with her.

When she emerged onto the platform, blinking to see in the stark light, where Pristina stood beside Fantomas and Toro, the three turned and looked on her with frowns. Cancer smiled and tossed her hair with a flick of her head. She wore a light blouse such as was popular among the more progressive Shaivist girls back in Salem, tucked into skin-tight Sterling-suit pants and boots. That alone would be an abomination to the Sunni slicks, the degree of their outrage dependant on their adherence to either the old earth Koran or the RK Mahdi's Illumination. If the later, Pristina and Fantomas would be quite upset.

Cancer held her smile, gazing at her mother.

"This is slick operations here on out, Cancer. You can't walk out here like a friggin' civie!" Toro wore her goggles over her eyes and held her violin case in one hand, the other hand splayed in her direction.

"Shut up, Toro. This is a joke," Cancer said, rolling her eyes.

Pristina stepped forward but Fantomas put a hand on her arm. That action on his part presaged an argument later between them. Cancer's eyes glittered, knowing.

"Look here, young lady. You will regret not prepping for planet-side. No oil, no goggles, no wet suit. Wearing clothes that are ill-suited at best and offensive at worst," he gestured at the partial Sterling-suit. "But these are your decisions. You will perform your duties. If I hear otherwise from Khalid you can forget about Salem next semester. It will be all on-station this year."

"What! You can't do that," Cancer said, hands crossed over her chest.

"Earn your keep. And it won't be an issue," Fantomas concluded, pulling his goggles from forehead over his eyes. His hair stood up, tied in a great knot atop his head. His beard dripped with oil.

Pristina turned away and walked to the railing without comment.

Toro stared at Cancer until she, too, turned with a desolate shaking of her head. Cancer wanted to punch her little sister but bit back on the urge, walking forward to stand beside her mom.

"Well?" Pristina said, not looking at her. Below them the slicks climbed onto a small shelf along the outer hull and squeezed into harnesses. The kelpies stood harnessed and strapped with safety lines for descent, their eyes shuttered to keep them calm. Cancer saw the first mate's boy, Amr, walking beside one of the fem slicks and climbing into a harness. Frigging sheep. His father and the slick foreman both climbed the ladder, eyes on Fantomas.

"I said ok," Cancer said to her mom. She knew the answer vague and easy to argue as to what, if anything, it actually entailed.

She felt her mother's eyes on her as the foreman and first mate stepped to their captain's side.

"Ready to drop," the foreman declared.

"How's Amr?" Fantomas asked and Khalid turned to the foreman.

"He'll do fine, gentlemen."

"Good," Fantomas said. Khalid nodded.

The captain turned toward the men and woman below and raised his fist in the air. Cancer narrowed her eyes. The slicks grew quiet, strapped to the far bulkheads. Then their own fists shot up with hoots and whistles until those sounds dissolved into a machismo cheer that even the animals joined.

Fantomas called out some jokes and bravado, riling everyone up. He ended with a paternal warning to safety and then the foreman took charge as the Captain and first mate stepped forward to the bridge.

"This is it, people..." the foreman bellowed in his wrecked voice.

"You two are apprentices to Khalid and the Captain," Pristina said, motioning after the two men. "Go on now." Cancer sneered at the gentle tone.

"Come on, Cancer," Toro squealed and ran after her daddy.

Cancer stalked back the way she had come, trailing her sister.

A few minutes later, after she sat secured in the bridge, *La Amenaza Elegente* dropped toward the planet, beginning its descent toward the place that would soon become its grave.

2

Taming the Megadolon

If on earth there be

a Paradise of Bliss,

It is this,

It is this,

It is this.

—Hakīm Abu'l-Qāsim Firdawsī Tūsī
(Pre-Mahdi Islamic Classics Collection, One Planet Era, also
quoted on the Shanam a polar monument, marking the failed
First Wave settlement)

*L*a *Amenaza Elegente* fell toward the moon, a miracle of Earth technology the moralities of Oasis must abide. The A-Grav layer allowed the ship to descend, allowed it to rise from the moon, much like the old Earth stories depicted but never thought through. It also allowed the ship-side gravity.

Other ships fell too, all toward the equatorial region and within a few minutes of each other. The ships coordinated loosely. Each drop sequence Hour One came such that within a month the landing sites would traverse the entire planet.

The AGL technology these ships used was just advanced enough to charge for return to orbit before High Tide. It was a curious effect of the economics driving slick captains that not a single human ship held station in orbit to assist should another ship have problems planet side.

From Shah Ferdowsi orbit, a Post-human He3 harvester, running innate heartbeat-monitoring of all AGL layers within several light-seconds, detected, in *La Amenaza Elegente's* pre-Hour One silence, a small device placed against *Amenaza's* AGL layer. After some analysis and queries, alerts tagged the human vessel.

The Post-human craft left orbit to intercept *La Amenaza Elegente.*

Amr followed Boski, hammering the stakes that she placed into the sand and then securing the mesh. The ship floated above them, a dark wedge threatening to fall on him at any moment, the ramp touching water and seabed. He smiled despite his predicament. The smell of brine and seaweed filled his sinuses, the water up to his thighs. *A bit deeper than normal* Boski warned him. The distant bleating of kelpies and the whine of 'foils filled the air as the other slick crews went about their duties. Some rode the 'foils in expanding circles, warding off unwanted beasts. The pitch of the vehicles drove much of the native fauna crazy.

Another of Boski's slicks splashed ahead of them, spooling out the orange mesh. Three more trudged around the other side of the ship and would meet them as they completed the corral.

Amr stared into the distance. The ship's one multifoil was anchored outside the corral near the ramp. Water undulated to the vanishing point in all directions, the clearest icy blue but for a band of water to the east that shone dark and emerald in Rigel Kent's light. A spire city loomed just a klick in that same direction, the term a misnomer for a pod of spire whales that had not kept up with the High Tide bulges. The formation meant kelpies for sure, scuttlebutt among the slicks implied.

"I guess that's why they're here too," Amr said, sliding his goggles onto his forehead and squinting against the glare. Near the spires another slick craft hung suspended above the water, its form more of an inverted tear drop than the angular tooth of *Amenaza*.

Boski turned toward him, her expression unreadable behind the goggles, and then out toward the spires and the other ship.

"Get back to work," she said. "And put your goggles on your eyes."

Amr did as she said. He liked her scoldings.

"And wipe the stupid smile off your face. Slicks don't smile."

He had to look away, playing at working extra hard, because her words made him grin all the more.

By the time their crew converged near the ramp leading into the main bay, slotting a gate into place, the Captain, first mate, the Captain's wife, and Toro stood on the ramp looking out at the waters. The ship's plane of gravity was at about forty-five degrees to the moon's, so he didn't realize who he saw from this angle wading down the ship's own reservoir and then up onto the ramp that curved out into the sea like a giant metal tongue. Cancer strode into full view, her eyes shut.

She wore no goggles and her skin did not shine with the prismatic gleam of kelpie oils. The Captain stared at her, shaking his head.

"Cancer, see here..." The Captain said then shook his head.

Khalid strode down the ramp into the water.

"Boski, hold here for a moment, please," his father said. His hair in tight braids, green brass goggles, wet suit, trident on his thigh, oiled skin glistening in the gloaming, comm lashed about his head: no man better illustrated "slick" than did Khalid. His father carried himself with a dignity born of his faith in God, but also in his loathing to side with either of the Sunni systems or the Shaivists. *Ours is to strive and to give thanks, not to divide wheat from chaff.* This made no literal sense to Amr, who did not know what wheat and chaff was, but he understood the gist.

He sank down into the water to rest on his haunches, but Boski slapped the back of his head.

"Don't do that, stupid." She said the word as if a "y" followed the "t."

Amr lurched to his feet, rubbing the back of his head, an irritated glance cast in Boski's direction. The other slicks, New Mahdi devouts shaved of all hair and plastered in equipment their fathers probably bequeathed them, waded off outside the corral to stand in a small huddle and stare outward. Amr thought, for some, Shanama could be a special place. A religious one; kind of like the Rub al-Ghali wastes back on Oasis.

"Perhaps Nilay will not have time for the apprenticeship," Khalid said quietly to Boski as he came close. "Providing no dishonor toward the foreman, would you be willing to take on the boy?"

"Sir, I'd be honored but... I'm just a slick," Boski said. *And just a woman*, Amr thought hung between them as well.

"Just a slick is just right. I'll clear it with the foreman. And you will be compensated in addition." He held up a hand at her protest on the final point and walked back up the ramp where he and the Captain whispered as the mother and oldest daughter stared each other down. Amr had missed their exchange.

Khalid stepped from the Captain and raised his head toward Cancer and Toro.

"All right, girls, you know how we recommend you outfit yourself. Are you both ready to proceed? Do you need a few minutes to finish getting ready?" Khalid held his hands as if in prayer while the Captain and ship's mum walked off in the most vexed, parental fashion, for a moment not Captain and wife but father and mother, struggling. These words represented indulgence unheard of among slicks and entailed real shame. Cancer crossed her arms, chin up and bare eyes now staring the first mate down. At least she wore the wet suit bottoms, Amr thought, but her light hair hung to her shoulders as if prepared for an afternoon stroll among the shops in Salem, white blouse already sticking to her stomach, and her skin was not oiled. Toro's face reddened as she listened and watched her big sister's defiance until she stepped to the first mate, a cross look marring her pretty, be-goggled face. Hair cut short and secured in a single knot atop her head, outfitted like a dwarf slick. Perfect but for the violin.

"See here, Mister Sujjad," Toro said to Khalid, echoing her father. "I'll not be lumped in with this dry civvy riff-raff. I am a slick girl and that's that. I am bringing my fiddle but the case latches on my back like so and I've had the instrument treated by Salem's best so it will not be hurt by these waters. I am ready, sir. To the mermen with *her*."

Amr wanted to smile at the child's outburst but Cancer's behavior disturbed him. Khalid leveled his eyes at Cancer.

"Let us go then, you and I. And you, fierce one," he said to Toro, patting the violin case that kept his hand from her back. Khalid led the girls and their father outside the corral to the multifoil, Pristina charging back into the ship.

"Boski, get your crew and follow us, please," Khalid called. Amr turned to her.

"Yes!" he clapped his hands, then composed himself.

"Shite," Boski hissed, goggles reflecting two perfect, enthusiastic doppelgangers of Amr that grew dismayed as the ship's mistress emerged from the bay atop a huge kelpie.

"Is the boy not ready for a 'foil?"

"No, mum. We've not trained on them yet."

"No worry. He can ride on Luchadora with

me," Pristina said.

Amr's heart sank. Oh, the indignity. It proved the first time he ever saw Boski smile.

"Thank you, mum," she said, beaming.

This would become their routine over the next several drops. After landing, while the slick crews ranged about for herds of kelpies and abbies, stray pontoon whales, schools of prigs, isopods, stromatolites, or any other megafauna that might have been stranded in low tide, Boski's crew set up the corral and then accompanied the Captain and first mate and their charges to investigate points of nearby interest before the real work began.

It was that first spire city with the inverted teardrop floating nearby that would stick with Amr, though.

The one where death first came calling.

With his hand around Pristina's stomach, Amr temporarily forgot his embarrassment and struggled not to grow excited behind her on the kelpie. That would prove embarrassing.

Kelpies functioned a bit like the unifoils, rising up out of the water on articulated tails to reduce drag, so that he and Pristina drifted far above the squat multifoil passenger platform on their trek out to the spire city. The kelpie was an oily, short-haired mammal and mounts like Luchadora were equipped with reins and saddles that tilted forward at forty-five degrees when the beasts were at rest, so that the saddles were horizontal at full bore.

Pristina had opted for a short haircut, rather than a shave, and Amr spent as much time staring at the nape of her neck as he did looking toward the spire whales. The sky, cloudless was a reflection of the sea, clearest azure with a horizon where heavens and sea melded into eternity.

Boski and the other slicks ranged ahead, behind, and to their sides, scanning for tape sharks and such.

"What if we find mermen in the city, momma!" Toro shouted from the multifoil. He felt the woman laugh. A steady spray cooled his face and legs. Toro must still think it an actual city.

A few minutes later they arrived at the base of the closest spire and Khalid brought the multifoil to a halt and anchored it while the slicks did the same with their 'foils. The loud droning echoed in his ears after their engines died.

A stronger sea-scent wafted in the air. It smelled good: less fishy and more of copper, soil, salt.

"You can slide off, mi ho," the Captain's wife said to him.

"Yes, mum. Thank you, mum."

"Amr."

"Yes?"

"When it is just you and I, Pristina is fine. When other slicks are around, this is good."

Amr nodded at her as she turned toward him. He understood 'this' was the formality he'd assumed. He offered a quick smile, lowered himself down from the saddle, and slid off the Kelpie's back. The tail lashed him into the water, sprawling, and he sucked in a mouthful of the briny soup before pushing back up to his feet.

The emerald waters were colder than the water back at the ship and he shivered in the breeze as it fingered him, as everyone getting out of the multifoil and the slick crew stared at him with expressions bemused, irritated, or indifferent. Cancer one of the latter.

The spires towered into the sky, thrice as tall as the greatest mosques back on Salem. Mother of pearl rainbows arced in the air between the spires and the many-chambered tubes spiraling up and around, armored in spikes and spines, colored in flat earth tones, lustrous metallics, and swaths of flesh-like membranes. While some of the spires pretended at fairy-tale castles, others were disturbingly phallic.

Pristina dropped a spike into the seabed to secure Luchadora, cooed to the beast, and shooed Amr toward Boski with a flick of her hand. He and the other sticks ranged ahead in a line as the group loped into the spire city. Over half of the spires were aptly named towers, while the remainder crowded in the water like giant blooms and fruiting bodies. A supine Buddha-ish formation lay to their side for a time, followed by a ship-sized fractal egg. Water lapped at the spires and a wind gusted out past them and back in again as if the pod of whales breathed in unison. Amr noticed vast orifices among some of the fractal folds and spines, usually at water level, sometimes not. And as often the openings sphinctered open wide and expelled a low moaning and a musk of deeper sea and sea life.

The canals meandered between the colossi, past a spire where grew a huge circular membrane that bulged and wrinkled with hidden movement. Amr hopped past, imagining a huge eye opening and then focusing on him.

Even after rounding a whale carapaced like a hill of dead trees the sense of being watched remained. Occasionally a shadow slid over Amr, or someone ahead of him.

"Are there birds on Nama?"

"Ghost sharks," the slick beside him said with a smirk. Ghost sharks, Amr, knew, could launch into the air and there remain aloft on updrafts, but High Tide was their domain. The statement mocked Amr.

Amr edged away from the slick, a pale-skinned Shaivist with passages from the Gitas inked into his arms and across his back, who stared at Amr and chuckled still. But then again, maybe Amr assumed. The goggles everyone wore still threw him: not being able to see people's eyes.

Later they heard the splashing and honks of a kelpie herd a few canals over, and soon after the sound of unifoils.

They walked for thirty minutes among the canals of that impromptu and nameless metropolis, until they stumbled upon a hatch of fledgling spire whales. Fat, car-sized bulges with no apparent spires, the creatures cried like Old Earth whales, voices high and uncanny, and surged away from these interlopers in their domain.

"Look, da— Captain!" Toro called, pointing toward the spire on the far side of the hollow place where the calves had huddled. The spire filled with light, a nautilus turned inside out and trapping the sun like honey or amber with veins of rose. At the base, the spire spread out in a flat bulge, an amphitheater to this gathering place.

The girl held her hands up and out, signaling silence. Even the slicks stopped talking once they noticed her.

"Hello," she said up into the folds and chambers that spoke her voice back to her, multiplied. "Ah, acoustics!"

Toro waded waist deep in the water over to where the formation connected to the spire and used the open chambers and crenelations to clamber onto the plateau. The child stood for a moment, water sluicing from her, then strode to the near edge and looked down at her audience. Amr stood toward the rear of the huddle with the other slicks, adapting to unspoken protective positioning. A shiny oil slick surrounded them like liquid rainbow. The Captain put an arm around his wife and she leaned her head on his shoulder for just a moment. Cancer glowered, her disgusted gaze alighting anywhere but on her sister.

Toro pulled the violin case from her back and laid it at her feet. She opened the case, pulled out the instrument and bow, and stood with the bow held dramatically and the violin propped against her neck.

"This is called 'Taming the Megadolon' by slick apprentice Toro Patton-Guerrero."

She frowned as she spoke, eyes half-closed, bow lowered to the instrument and sliding back and forth, first slow and then with growing intensity. Amr thought the song sad, but then it phased, paused, redoubled, now forlorn, then defiant, until the tempo morphed and rose frantic, high, urgent, settling into a staccato declaration and finally a one-two, one-two, one-two coda that Toro allowed to fade into silence.

"Salute!" the slick beside Amr called, one of the New Mahdi Sunnis. Everyone in the small group laughed, the Captain's guffaw echoing among the walls around them.

Just then a shadow fell on the child.

Fantomas' voice choked with a garbled scream: *Toro!* And Amr sensed more than saw the father's rush toward his girl. Behind her grinning face, feet hung suspended. Above that, slender silhouetted legs, torso, arms balancing, head tilted toward the child. A Sterling-suit. Earth, certainly. Post-human. The Abomination that compelled the initial exodus to Rigel Kent. The periodic summits out in the RK Kuiper belt meant continued contact with Sol system, and the pact between species meant both could harvest He3 from Shah Ferdowsi. They, Post-humans, were not supposed to be here, on Shanama.

The father shrieked at his daughter, who wasted precious seconds on her haunches, pressing the instrument and bow into case, closing the lid, and throwing the latches.

Pristina hauled Cancer back from the ledge, Khalid stood beside the Captain, calling Toro to hurry, his arms out-stretched. The world slowed. The other slicks stood in the same spots, but now their arms outstretched toward the black figure, pistols in hand.

Boski, when Amr first suited up with the extra slick gear, took his gun away, but then gave it back, safety engaged but loaded. *You're a slick. You carry it like anyone else. You don't take it out unless Mara himself has jumped out of the sea to take you.* It was an odd statement for a Shaivist. Surprise, at the slow clicking passage of time, at the thoughts, at the gun in his hand, at the cold way in which he disengaged the safety, took aim. The two fathers pulled the girl from the shelf and time sprang back into motion with a bark and the smell of gunpowder. The silhouette fell to the shelf, clutching its chest, with a muffled, electronic cough.

Smoke wafted from Amr's pistol. His ears rang. He lowered the weapon and wanted to cry at the stares that met him. Goggled eyes in pale faces.

"Safety on, holster it, and lead the ship mistress back," Boski shoved, splayed hand on his chest, and motioned at the other slicks, some to go with him, some to stay with her.

Pristina pushed Cancer toward Amr much the same way Boski had just pushed him away. She surged back and grabbed Toro, carried her several seconds and then lowered her into the water, urging her on, hand in hand. Two other slicks ranged ahead and lingered just behind, guns at the ready.

"Well, boy," Cancer said. She must have fallen, hair wet, eyes red from the briny water, cotton blouse plastered to her breasts. "You just fired the first shot in an interstellar war. And this your first day as a slick. Good job." Smile sweet as her eyes glittered.

Amr stopped at a bend beside the psuedo-

Buddha and waved the other slicks on out of sight. There he vomited into a crevice at water-level.

"Sorry," he said afterward, a small prayer-handed bow to the Buddha-whale. Then he turned back toward the empty canal behind him.

"Sorry," he repeated with the same bow. He hurried to catch up with the others.

Pristina had the two girls mount Luchadora with her, Toro in front of her, Cancer behind. She spurred the beast into action, tilting up out of the water and jetting away as the other two slicks revved their 'foils and raced to catch up.

"Guard the multifoil," Pristina commanded as they whisked away.

The two foils followed the kelpie toward the distant smear of the Amenaza. They soon left Amr in a quiet that spoke in lapping waves and the groaning of shifting spire whales. Amr stood thigh-deep in the water and realized how alone he was, turning in a slow circle and scanning the water around him, the pale sand at his feet where pebbles and shells shifted in minute currents. Here and there were sprigs of seaweed and carbuncle growths he did not recognize.

Leaning against the multifoil, contemplating climbing aboard and waiting out of the water, the voices reached him. Not shouting nor idle conversation, but a miasma of chatter, a legion of voices tinged with an electronic buzz as though heard over the radio back in Oasis orbit. Listening, turning one way then the other, Amr realized the wind blowing in from around the small cove carried the cacophony. Curious, he pushed out from the craft and walked several meters out from the cove, passing out of the lee of the last spirewhale, the black teardrop sliding into view. The other slick ship.

But it was not a slick craft, he saw now. It was not a ship at all, in his understanding of the word. Tagging the control bead with a quick glance into his periphery, he dialed up the magnification on his goggles with a series of winks, and honed in on the mass of black Sterling-suits, crawling amid each other in the inverted tear drop. No ship or internal structure apparent, replaced by a writhing mass of bodies. periodically one drifted from the point at the bottom and slid into the water to follow a line of figures already walking toward Amr. A dozen on the ground so far, he judged, the nearest maybe twenty meters out.

Shite.

Amr reached down and felt the gun handle, backing away from the approaching figure. He thought of getting in the multifoil and going back for the others, or leaving them. That last thought shamed him and he shook his head that he'd even think such a cowardly thing. He thought to just run away, as best as he could run in this shallow sea, either away into the deep blue forever, or back to the group.

He backed into the multifoil and stood, transfixed, until that first figure neared him and then came along side. It stopped and turned its head toward him.

As if from a million miles away, the tinny voice spoke to him.

"Your AGL layer has an attached dampening device," neutral, male, tired, full of static.

The figure turned and walked on just as several slicks came surging into the cove from the direction of the ship, easing their 'foils into the water. The lead rider flung his 'foil aside and surge into Amr, grabbing him by both arms. The slick towered over him, first tilting Amr to the side, away from the Post-humans, and then pressing his face close, mouth breathing hard, goggles encrusted in green, hair a short, military crew. The gravel voice hit him.

"What did it say?" The foreman shook him for emphasis.

"What did it say, boy?"

"I shot one of them," Amr felt his mouth curl around the words, curdling into a sob.

The foreman shook him again, one handed, then lashed his palm across Amr's face. The smack silenced Amr and drained the blood from his face.

"Damping device," not understanding the Post-human words, or the foreman, or even his own brain at that moment. The foreman pulled him closer, so like Boski, but so different, rough face and green-caked goggles, teeth yellowed, breath hot and sour.

"Not a word, boy. Not to anyone. No panic among the crew because of any more of your mistakes. Yes?"

"Yes. Yes sir."

The next bit would remain a blur to Amr. They scooted out of there in the multifoil, lingering long enough to see the Post-humans trudge out of the maze with their fallen comrade. Their reprisal an occasional glance, leveled at Amr. He believed. When they arrived back at *Amenaza*, operations persevered, crews bringing in kelpie herds and other beasts.

Nilay put Amr to work outside the cordon, guiding beasts into the gate and up the ramp. Amr thought his father or the Captain would discuss what happened. He thought they'd have questions about the Post-human drone and his message. He thought he'd be in Boski's charge, but for the rest of that drop and the next five Amr knew little but constant labor and the stench of all those watery kelpie and assorted crawling, splashing creatures. Thorny scales, slick hides, chitin and shell. Even through the gloves, wet suit, and the layer of oil, the ocean and its bounty did their best to inundate him. To scar him.

At some point a couple drops and maybe four hours sleep later, he chanced past Cancer after working with Nilay and some other slicks securing the corral. She had not relented, and still wore the Sterling-suit bottoms (he now recognized) and cotton top, her hands puckered and red, face and lips blistered. It startled him to gaze on naked eyes.

"The good slick boy. Killed anyone lately, slick boy?" And with that she and her eyes left the ramp and trekked back into the ship.

Each drop they went exploring with the family, then back to the ship and roughly fourteen hours labor before the water started pulling at them, portending high tide. They'd batten up, secure the beasts that filled the main and tertiary holds, the Captain would varyon the AGL, and up they'd go into orbit and then dock with various transfer orbitals to sell livestock that would both feed the orbital community and the surplus sold to Oasis in their perigee.

Nilay kept Amr on a short leash until the seventh drop. Then things went all to hell.

3
The Celebration

No matter how far I drift

Deep waters (Deep waters)

Won't scare me tonight.
—Portishead, Deep Waters
(from the Dar al-Salam archives of Pre-Spike Earth culture)

Drop seven, and night on Shanama. In opposition, Beta hung in the sky and rendered the eve in deep blues with enough light to read by. The slick crews set out on their initial recon and the family headed for a small stand of spires.

Along with the comm strapped to Pristina's shaved head, she wore a camera on loan from Dar-al-Salam University. She started filming in the spire whale pod they'd visited on drop one: footage of the majesty of the whales, Toro's innocent performance, and the chaos that followed. Riding out of the cove on Luchadora, Toro in front of her and Cancer behind, she'd glanced north to the inverted teardrop hovering just beyond the pod. She still poured over those seconds. It did not appear to be a ship when magnified, but a writhing mass of Sterling-suits.

What she had intended to call *Hearts of Darkness* would need a new name, but with that image to tie into her examination of the spire whale and kelpie relationship wrapped around the drama of slick life and labor, she suspected the provost would be quite happy with the documentary. Better understanding of the Shanama ecosystem could lead to lesser dependence on Earth technology, a cultural triumph the Oasis city-states coveted. The endeavor represented a huge revenue stream for the University and hence a focal point of research and development for many of the departments.

Once upon a time, a research position in the biology division had been her goal. Maybe she'd complete her doctorate and take up instruction, she had thought. But then Fantomas careened, literally, into her life and rent all those plans asunder.

She had no regrets. And Pristina felt happy to play ship mum beside her Captain. But, research assignments from the University represented something that was hers and hers alone, and she needed that. The film was a personal triumph. Or would be.

"*A Triumph of Will*. How does that sound, Boski?"

"For the film, Mum? Good. I like it."

"I need to check and see if that was used back on Earth or I'll have to put up with your Captain's scorn."

Boski smiled and nodded. The woman wore a

few dull metallic loops in her braids, a small concession to femininity.

Two slicks ranged ahead of them among molted isopod exoskeletons and prigs, the later the adolescent phase of spire whales in the form of irregular domes about three meters tall. The translucent exoskeletons refracted the light and drifted in the waist-deep water, light flotsam knocking husk to husk across the square kilometer and creating an atmosphere much different than the spire cities they had found on the six prior drops. Scraping and echoes filled the air along with the lapping of water and distant kelpie calls. The skeletons and prigs smelled of rust, gunpowder, and rot. In the distance, near the center of the skeleton field stood a half dozen proper spire whales.

Behind Boski and her waded the girls, Fantomas, Khalid, and Nilay with Amr and two other slicks.

Looking back, she saw Amr edging forward, near his father when Nilay grabbed him by the arm.

"Go back and guard the 'foils, *bakhara*," Nilay said to him.

Pristina met Khalid's eyes.

Amr stopped, crestfallen, and turned without comment to trudge back the way they'd come.

"Leave it be, Mum," Boski said, following her attention.

"Of course," Pristina put her hand against a isopod husk as she passed. It felt like hard plastic or glass. She clicked it with her gloved fingers.

"He's doing well." She seemed ready to say

more but left it at that.

"I thought you were going to take him on," it wasn't a question. Her underclothes chafed her inner thighs. She shook her head thinking of how uncomfortable Cancer must be. Stubborn girl.

"After the incident on drop one..."

"Did you lose the lead position?"

"Yes, mum."

"You'll be compensated for your help to me with the documentary. I'll be including you in the credits as my personal assistant."

"Not necessary—"

"None of that, Boski. Come on. Look... Familiar? Yes?" She surged through the water, smiling up at the spires. All six towered like mosques into the dark, cloudy sky, chambered, twisted, nightmare-cathedrals that they were. Four had bases that spiraled out into flat shelves like that Cancer had stood upon. One dipped so low that it served as a basin where a few fish swam but the other three butted against each other, creating a dry, raised area large enough to host a ball game; just mind the edges.

By the time Pristina hopped across to the last shelf the others stepped from the first water-filled base and onto dry shell. Boski walked to the pink wall of one of the spires and knelt, Toro at her side. She would mark the whale with a permanent tag. She painted on the red numerals and then twisted to Pristina.

"Is it okay, Mum?" She ticked her head toward Toro, who held the brush.

"What will you put on it, Toro?" Pristina asked with a smile. The girl still had her belly, but it was just that age. She never stopped. Nor did her enthusiasm. She had just enough hair to keep it tied atop her head in imitation of her father.

Toro smiled back and answered by laying the paint tool to chitin and drawing a squat "T" nested inside a fat, lazy "U." A stylized bull's head.

Her daughter swiveled.

"My sign!"

Pristina nodded. Cancer stalked close and shook her head in disgust.

She heard raised voiced and turned. The men lingered in a group beside the pool on the first shelf, confabulating.

She loitered near, pretending more interest in the spires than the men.

"Something the matter?"

"No. No. Not at all," Fantomas answered, his shock of hair still bound at the top of his head, so that he seemed forever surprised. "Nilay has the idea to take a few hours toward the end of the drop to have a cook-out for the slicks."

"You're quite concerned for the morale, eh?" Pristina said. "Sounds like a good idea," looking from the blank slate of Nilay's face to her perplexed husband.

"I thought so, ma'am," Nilay inclined his head.

"Boski and I will set up our equipment here. Leave one of the 'foils by Luchadora—"

"You'll spend the whole drop here?" Fantomas asked. It would be fourteen hours by the time they returned to the ship.

"We'll be fine. Send one of the crews around hour eleven and we'll help set up for dinner. Hour twelve. Have each slick bring what they want.

We'll have the fire going."

One of the whales listed in the water, as dead as the skeletal field that surrounded the six spires. It remained erect thanks to the wide shelf at its base and the water that had flooded the open chambers therein. A round orifice in the shell reposed at water level. Pristina led Boski in, switching on the light mounted along with the camera on her head, and high stepping into the water that was both colder and smelled saltier than that outside. After slipping on the spire's internal lip, she stood thigh-deep in the water, sand and muck squishing in her booted footsteps. Clumps of hair and scales floated in the water along with a few soggy turds.

"Stinks like kelpie," Boski said.

Even without the camera's light, the meager light from outside filled the space with a gloaming whisper of illumination.

"But look," Pristina pointed toward the internal apex of the spire. Boski breathed a slight *oh*. Above them the shell spiraled up and up into infinity. An open space ascended all the way up, more like mosque or cathedral than ever.

"Hello," Pristina called up into the space and it answered back in myriad echoes.

The water's stench faded in the holiness of that space.

"The stair effect indicates chambers spiraling up," She looked around and saw the shelf clinging to the spire wall and descending on her left into the water. The only open chamber, the ramp spiraling across three-fourths of the wall and up a

good ten meters before the next chamber.
Another orifice, oval, gaped into the next
chamber.

"Yes?" Boski asked.

"Oh yes,' Pristina grinned at the other woman.
Boski was barely older than Cancer, she realized
for the first time. Slick life hardened a woman.
Cancer would do well to act more like this one.

They leared into the slope and scampered up
to the portal Sponge-barnacles clotted the incline,
making for an easy ascent. Pristina clambered into
the chamber and leaned against the lower wall
while Boski entered. The outer shell thinned to
translucence about halfway up the three meter
high space, giving them a glimpse of Beta
sparkling in the sky and shattering into a billion
flashes of light in the ocean below. The
translucent membrane circled up at the same
incline as the chamber and Pristina extrapolated
that the higher chambers would be likewise
illuminated.

Boski trundled up the inclined chamber and
poked her head into the next, her voice echoed
into silence. "You're right, mum."

They spent several hours climbing from
chamber to chamber, up and around. The first six
showed signs of kelpie habitation. Pristina
trembled as she filmed, narrating on the fly. She
had Boski pick up a patch of molted hair and
scales, a bone, and some small teeth. They even
stumbled upon a small carcass.

"Calf," Boski said, tipping it with her booted
toe.

"So, it's easy enough to see the benefit of the

relationship to the kelpies..."

"High tide," Boski nodded.

"Yes. But what about the whales?" Pristina wondered aloud.

"Maybe they help get the prigs out?"

Pristina just nodded. For Boski to hazard a guess said much about the trust formed between them. She'd not risk offense critiquing the suggestion.

She had Boski go back to the ship and retrieve the other battery for the camera and some tracking tags.

While she waiting she back-tracked and went back over each of the preceding chambers in slow, careful swathes of the camera, noting details she'd over-looked earlier, taking samples of the translucent shell and the sponge-barnacles on the floor.

When Boski returned, Pristina thanked her and planted one of the tags in the first segmented chamber.

"Why, mum?"

"We'll tag the other five, which are living, and this will give us a control for understanding what their migration patterns are contrasted with what the high tide bulges force upon the spires."

Up, they climbed as the chambers grew more level and more diverse. Chitin tubes snaked upon the walls and terminated in this chamber in a series of basins, the next in a gaping hole in the outer shell. The air in the chambers grew dry and dusty.

Channels filled the surface of another chamber, looking like nothing so much as a giant brain turned inside out. The next —and they were nearing the apex, the rooms smaller and the outer curve more pronounced— held a chitin mound that served as a nice bench Pristina rested on, and a full translucent wall where Boski stood and surveyed the sea.

"Oh, shite," Boski put her hands on the outer shell, staring down.

"What?"

"The cooking crew is already here," Boski said.

"What time is—" She reached up and tweaked the side of her goggles, turning on her heads up display.

"Thirty after eleven. We're late."

Pristina didn't care. Except for Boski.

"Go on down. I'm right behind you, dear."

"You're certain, mum?"

Pristina nodded.

After Boski left, Pristina made pace up and through the remaining chambers, sweeping her head back and forth, up and around, taking it all in. She'd do this once per chamber with the light on, and again with it off, slowing down as best she could in her excitement. Under the harsh light science would find its best work, but in the blue-tinged gloam she would find her viewer's hearts.

The last dozen chambers altered in structure, folding back from the outer shell in a honeycomb of interconnected cubes, globes, and laddered oblongs. Detritus filled them as well. Small seashells and pebbles. Seaweed, megalodon teeth as big as her head, mats of kelp. It wasn't until she turned and stared upon the drawings on the wall that realization erupted in her mind. She stood in the top-most chamber lit from above by light through the translucent chitin. Flesh-colored and brown-speckled walls, with dark-brown and red paintings of fish, kelpie, spires, kraken, megalodons, and slick ships.

Mermen lived in spire whales.

She walked bent-backed through three chambers until she reached one lower and against the outer shell. Camera on, light off, she edged close to what she already thought of as a window and looked down at the huddle of slicks working at the cooking pots below. Then she looked out to the *Amenaza* in the distance, that black tooth hanging in the air.

HUDs on, she dialed up the magnification on the camera and could make out a commanding figure walking among slicks. Setting this group off on their 'foils, and now that one. Calling to someone in the ship, inspecting the haul of a last crew coming in with a couple dozen head of kelpie. Pats on the back and orders barked. That latter at a smaller, tentative figure always at the other's side.

She stood and watched this for some time, until even the multifoil with its glut of small figures set off leaving the final two alone.

"I swear to Allah, Nilay..." she hissed aloud, unaware. But after entering the ship he emerged a few minutes later with a pat for the boy's back followed by a walk together to two remaining 'foils. They talked for just a moment. No— it wouldn't be conversation. It would be Nilay talking and the boy listening. Then Amr nodded and set off on the 'foil in her direction. The other lingered a moment to turn and stare up at the ship. He saluted the vessel before he mounted his 'foil and followed.

By the time she stepped from the spire-hole and out into the blue half-light, the smell of grilled fish tickled her nose accompanied by the laughter of slicks standing around pots where shrimp and tiny isopods boiled with salt and spices. A few battery-operated lamps stood on poles with garish streamers draped between them in an attempt at festivity. One of the slicks, a man covered in tattoos of script from the Gitas with a lariat hung across his shoulders, sat playing a small woodwind while one of his fellows, an RK Mahdi-follower judging by his total shave and the treated copy of the Illumination hanging at his waist, strummed through chords on his guitar.

The wind picked up for a moment. It usually did toward the end of the drop, harbinger of high tide and the storms accompanying the bulges. Ozone mixed with the smell of salt, brine, and seaweed, wafting among the savory smoke of the grill and the steam from boil pots.

Fantomas belly-laughed amid the lights, gabbling with the newer slicks. Trying to make them less new, more known. A few sat in folding chairs near the Captain, but most lounged on the shelf, eating from plates balanced in their laps or set beside them on the chitin floor. Khalid walked among the men and few women, encouraging them to eat and drink. Bowing to each with a small prayer as he was given to do.

Cancer sat alone on the far side, nearest the

established approach through the field of prigs and isopod shells, her feet dangling in the waters contained in the first shelf. A few slicks floated there as though it were a sauna. Toro sat near her sister, ignored.

Glancing across the small party, one diminutive slick stood useless guard ten meters out near the start of the isopod husks. Pristina clenched her fists, her jaw, when she saw Nilay step to Cancer's side and call the boy.

A few minutes later, after Amr stocked his plate and Nilay absconded the boy of his attention and joined the other slicks, she allowed herself to relax. She stepped gingerly among splayed hands and plates to her husband. Kissed him. Hugged Khalid who had arrived back at the Captain's side, and then she drifted toward the cook pots with a dour look for the foreman who sat to the other side of the Captain.

Boski met her at the cook pots with a smile.

"What can I get you, mum?"

"Whatever's good, yes?"

Boski nodded and filled a plate with a variety of fish: blackened, curried, and boiled. The smell made Pristina's stomach ache she was so hungry. Someone even provided a plate of bhakarvadi, small spicy-sweet biscuits for dunking in coffee or tea.

"Two plates, if you will."

Boski filled a second plate with the same and held it out to Pristina. Sweat beaded the slick woman's face and Pristina regarded her eyes, the goggles hanging around her neck.

"That's yours. Come join me," Pristina said.

With another nod, Boski followed her to the far reaches of the light, on the last shelf where a few slicks lay beside empty plates, resting. They ate in silence until Boski looked at her. Pristina had her goggle around her neck too. "What is it, mum?"

The slick musicians had started playing again, surrounded by a small audience of clapping, laughing, shouting slicks. A few danced in the light near the three men in charge.

"After you left. I went all the way up. You know it is a silly thing that we call the whale pods spire cities, yes?"

"Of course."

"But I found signs of habitation. At least in a dead spire like this one, mermen live in them."

Boski sucked the guts from one of the boilers and then ate the body. "That's a big find. University will be happy."

Toro startled Pristina just then.

"Mom," The girl still wore her goggles and looked very serious. Amr trailed a few feet behind her.

"Yes, mi ha?"

"I want to play with the other slicks. Can I go get my violin?"

"You forgot it?"

"No, ma'am, the luthario back in Salem, Dar al-Salam I mean, told me to treat the wood so often, so I did. I didn't know they'd be playing." The girl's chubby face contorted in disgust.

"It's not so big a deal, mi ha. Just enjoy yourself."

"Excuse me, mum," Amr shifted behind Toro.

"I can take her back to the ship if you like."

"We don't have that much time left to the cook out, Toro," Pristina raised her eyebrows and tilted her head. She winked at Amr. The boy didn't blush or smile. The last few drops had changed him.

"Please, mom."

The music transformed the cookout into a proper party. The slicks clapped and cheered dancers and the two musicians. One of the other women did a belly dance that enthralled everyone and Pristina heard Boski mutter, *that's a bad idea.*

"Amr, take the multifoil. You're good to drive it now, yes?"

"Yes, mum."

"Toro, tell your sister I said to go with."

"Thank you, *mum.*" Toro's smiled beamed at her and after a moment's hesitation she leaned over and hugged both her and Boski. That did elicit a smile from Amr, and he strolled away with an arm around Toro to find her sister. Boski laughed.

"She's a good girl," she said.

"And he's a good boy," Pristina added.

"No, mum. He's a man now. Has to be," Boski took another bite from her plate, eyes down.

Pristina expected Cancer to arrive in the next few minutes with complaints, but she didn't. Maybe she, like Amr, was growing.

The revelry escalated in the best of ways. Pristina had seen celebrations planet-side before and they had a tendency to go awry. Everyone behaved, even in wake of the belly dance.

"Close call, that," Boski suggested, sounding like a matriarch.

"You need to get to know my oldest. Maybe you'll rub off"

The slick woman shifted her head and looked at Pristina.

"Ah. You know: influence her for the good," Pristina clarified.

"Oh, yes. Yes, ma'am. I can try. *Rub off,*" she tested the phrase. "Maybe I can rub off on her." Her smile shone bright in the deep blue night. They laughed.

Sensing that festivities would wind down soon, they rose to join the circle surrounding the dancers and players, and joined in the clapping. Boski whistled with two fingers in her mouth and Pristina hollered on a troupe of slicks performing an intricate acrobatic dance. The sounds echoed among the six spires just enough to amplify the ruckus between gales billowing in from tideward.

She spied Nilay approach before, she suspected, he realized his destination. His gaze vacillated, initially aloof, but soon betraying urgency, as it scoured the revelers. He circled the gathering, edging closer to her, still searching, unaware of her attention. She recalled the salute he'd offered the ship before departing. The music, clapping, and laughter continued, but Nilay's tightening visage consumed her. Her pulse and breath quickened.

Pristina stopped clapping and, eyes fixed on the foreman, strode toward him. The lights filled the space between spires with an indestructible yellow joy. Or the voices and music created that.

Her husband's voice along with Khalid's rose and fell in jubilation. Among men who had done honest labor in their charge. Or so they thought.

She felt Boski's hand on her back. She, too, knew something was wrong. If only from Pristina's demeanor.

As she came into dyad with Nilay, he still did not notice. His gaze drifted inward toward the light and dancers, out among the audience, then faltered on her.

"Amr. Have you seen the boy?"

Pristina crossed her arms. "I have."

His shoulders fell a bit and he sighed. In the dim, the light from the celebration cast a ruin of shadows on his neck. His voice sounded full of liquid. Or fear.

"Good. Good. I need to talk to him—"

"But you can't, Nilay," Pristina said.

"You said—"

"He's taken the girls, both my daughters, back to *Amenaza*." She didn't have to ask. He paled at the words, his shoulders burdened again, his chest filling with air. Nilay veered one way, then the other, then rotated away from her and ran across the shelves and vaulted into the water, thrashing his way to the 'foils.

"Shite," Pristina hissed and ran after him, Boski in tow.

The others continued in their celebration, unaware, until the ship sirens sounded and dopplered into the distance, alerting them all to the certainty of their abandonment before the coming of high tide on Shanama.

The sirens, alone, did not worry Amr.

"Who's still on the ship?" he asked the girls as they trudged up the curve of the ramp into ship-side gravity.

Toro shook her head, Cancer ignored him.

"Go get your damn violin, Tor," she said instead.

Whoever sounded the siren better have a good reason or they'd be in for it.

Toro started off in a corridor between animal corrals in the water-filled bay. The girl moseyed like an old slick. Once an affectation, it seemed real now. The life wearied even a kid like her. He shook his head. She glanced back at her sister, irritated he felt certain, when she stopped, turned, and stared.

"What's your problem?" Cancer said, easing down onto the raised ledge leading from bay to ramp. Toro's head tilted and her brow crinkled. "Toro!"

The girl started and raised a pointed finger outward, behind Cancer. Amr turned and stared, not understanding. Why did the water flow so fast? He stepped forward toward the ramp as Cancer stood, turned, hesitated. As she stepped up out of the water to descend the ramp realization dawned and he grabbed her arm and yanked her back from the edge.

"What the hell are you doing?" She screamed, leaning in to him and pushing his chest in a dare. A face close to his no longer moved him. Not so easily.

"We're moving, *apprentice*," he said. "Stay away from the ramp. Toro, the bridge." He didn't know what he'd do once he got there, or what help Toro would be, but it felt right.

He high-stepped through the water, past the honks of wild kelpies and trilling of abbies. A pontoon whale lay near the metal deck, rotating in place. He hit the transmit key at his shoulder on the 27MHz band they used to talk among crews, but no one answered. His codex would link with their satellite, but he didn't take it with him during drops. The comm in the bridge would have the same connection. Yes. That would be the answer. Father or the Captain could tell him how to stop the ship and get back to them. Amr smiled. This would be how he recovered from the mess of the last seven drops.

Toro fell behind but he heard her wheezing in his wake as he mounted the stairs two at a time and charged down the main access corridor, sluicing water and kelpie oil, a mad smile on his face.

"Everything's going to be fine," he breathed to himself. But he climbed the twangy ladder and emerged into the bridge where his hope and heart sank. The ladder twanged again and Toro bumped into him and seized his arm.

"The comm," the kid said, pointing. She caught his expression. "What's wrong?"

"Look," he said and nodded.

She gazed out toward the vastness of storm clouds, sea, and a distant line that represented the first of the little bulges. Beyond, a darkness beneath the storms obscured the mid and big bulges.

Amr wiped his face, oil, water, and despair

refusing to leave his visage.

"I know the ship's moving—"

"Toro. Think about how the ship is oriented planet-side. What should we see out the forward port?"

"Just the sky," she whispered.

"Just the sky," he agreed. He realized how like Boski he sounded that moment. Odd. "Something is wrong with the AG layer. And we're heading into high tide."

The ladder twanged and Cancer pushed past them.

"Why aren't you on the comm yet?" She strode across the bridge and picked up the receiver. Sighed, head down. She hit the all-hands channel.

"Ok. This is Cancer. We're on the bridge. Tell me how to turn this thing around."

4
Deep Waters

Faith is, at one and the same time, absolutely necessary and altogether impossible.
—Stanislaw Lem
(European States Collection, Dar al-Salam Pre-Spike Earth Library)

The foreman mounted a lone nearby unifoil, jetting off across the cove surrounding the platforms, and dodged into the maze of prigs and isopod husks, the 'foil leaving a wake of drifting skeletons and echoed whines as the rider revved, shifted, accelerated. The dawn painted the world in amber tones so like a dream. The beauty enraptured for a moment as she ran in the thigh-deep water after the man, the medium pulling at her, slowing her. Motes from some aerial life spun like tiny stars in galactic whorls, caught in the light and casting long, pin-thin bolts of shadow. Behind her, the spires loomed before a sky bruised gray and violet among mushrooming anvils full of rumbling and rain. In front of her Alpha blinded, for a time.

Pristina whistled for Luchadora and heard the animal shriek in the distance. She'd wrangled Luchadora before she'd given birth to Toro, taming the animal as a wild fawn. First as a pet, then as a mount. The animal recognized something in her mistress' voice, negotiating the husks and emerging wild-eyed and screaming to circle Pristina protectively. Mounting the beast, she stroked its trembling hide and dug her heels into its flanks.

With screams from rider and kelpie, they lifted up out of the water and streaked into the cleared path left behind by the 'foil.

Alpha, fat on the far horizon, momentarily blinded her as they emerged into open sea. The clouds tumbled from massive anvils in the east, rushing to block out the star as it ascended.

Nilay raced toward empty sky where the *Amenaza* had hung and Pristina followed. They'd landed close to the spires this drop.

The unifoil's whine died as he arrived ahead of her.

Luchadora bore full speed toward the tiny figure. Behind her Boski sped on her own 'foil and others would follow, alerted by the sirens. The AGL made no noise, and she could still see the ship streaming across the water toward storms, high tide, and the bulges, quiet as a nightmare.

She felt for both her blades, ready to show this hard man that she was no soft civie maid of Salem's intellectual elite. The flesh of her face stretched thin over her skull, the spray cool, a terrible grin contorting her features out of true, any tears lost to the wind and the sea water. Far off in the direction of her children the sky cracked in a great fracture of light, a rumble tumbling across rough waters like an afterthought. The megacumulous towered high and captured the growing daylight, even as they shattered with lightening. Little scraps of cloud already filled the sky above Pristina, caught in shadow or transmogrified into mirrors of the morning's glory and sweeping fast on the heels of low tide.

A white discoloration led his sight toward the receding speck of *Amenaza*. He neared its starting point, the parallax motion washing him with a brief moment of dizziness. The megacumulous loomed in the distance, ablaze with Alpha's dawn.

Spray in his face, Nilay thought of his father. His father, flesh locked away from him forever beneath the Sterling-Suit. Voice masked in tinny radio sounds. There was a time, as a child, that they'd played ball on a scratched-out field outside of Salem or wrestled on the floor at the collectivist common room.

He lost that particular hope long ago. Something to put aside. But there was this, now. This yearning that this not be so. That he'd not been duped into doing a right thing that destroyed.

Like father, like son.

Amenaza's wake bubbled still, mimicking the emotion that lingered on the surface of his mind.

Hope.

Hope that he'd not just murdered three innocents. Murder never his intention. Not so much as a bruise of harm to anyone on the *Amenaza* ever belonged to his plans.

He brought the 'foil to a stop, dropping it in the choppy water. Already he'd spied a ray and a small ghost shark. He lurched in the water a few steps, came to a standstill. The rumbling of thunder in the distance did not penetrate the silence in his head.

The waters around him surged, lapped, receded, flowed as if he stood in the surface of a waking beast. Alpha's light caught the severe wave tips in a million sparkling daggers that morphed before his eyes into long, crystal clear swathes of sunlight caught in the sea. Raindrops carried by the wind periodically hit those smooth expanses of light and marred them on impact.

His hope died.

None of the kids remained, and so he had killed them.

Nilay stood there, oblivious, as the ship's mum charged near, launched from her kelpie, and took him down into the brine, knives drawn, a slick black-clad maiden of deadly redemption.

Redemption would not be his.

The sobs that wracked him masqueraded as choking. He gulped the water, wanting the darkness of drowning, but his body rebelled. It wanted life.

Her face, as his body stilled, hung above him like a private sky, filled with a different sort of storm. A blade poised high, ready to strike.

Boski grabbed her wrist just as Pristina prepared to gut her children's killer.

"Mum, no," but Pristina screamed and yanked the blade toward the man's throat. He had given up, she could see, and it would be an easy kill. "Pristina." Strange, she would think later, how a simple transgression such as that could cut through the rage. She looked at Boski.

Her eyes ringed red behind the goggles. A girl

in many ways. Young, closer to Cancer's age than her own. Yet she'd made her way as a slick. Did she have family back on Dar al-Salam? Despite the time they'd spent together, she knew little of Boski.

"Move aside, mum," she commanded. Commanded. She took the knife from her hand, grabbed Nilay by the arm, and promptly twisted it behind his back and pushed him to his knees. In one swift motion she cut his wet suit from upper torso, stretched it away from the expanse of his back and then drew the blade across the mocha-colored skin, leaving a weeping gash from right shoulder to the top of his left buttock.

She shoved him forward into the water. He rose and turned on her.

"What the hell?" He yanked his goggles down around his neck, one hand behind his back, the other feeling for his own blade.

"No Nilay," Pristina stepped forward, between the man and Boski, though Boski edged alongside her. "I ask the questions. The ship. Tell me now."

Nilay glanced behind her. She could hear unifoils racing toward them.

"Abomination," he said. It explained a lot. She wondered if he'd always thought that way, or if he'd grown into it.

"Shite," Boski hissed. "You're one of *those.*"

He spit into the water and met the young woman's gaze.

"I'm not an ideologue. I know what will happen if we keep using the AGL and other Earth tech. Nama isn't a natural world. They seeded it. That's why the Earth DNA. You and your *implications.* It's their AG tech that causes the bulges. If not for them we could have settled Nama. We'd have no need for—"

"The ship, Nilay," Pristina repeated.

"The AGL has been reprogrammed. It will take them to the Big Bulge apex and then shut down. The ship will sink."

"Can you—"

"There is no undoing it. No shutting it off. No redirecting the ship."

"And—" Pristina stopped. They all knew he'd chosen the exact time when no ship on planet or in orbit could reach the vessel. None had remained in orbit and the one's still planet-side would only have enough charge to get back to orbit. "The ship won't sink. It's buoyant."

"No. The main hold doors are stuck open."

"We'll—"

"No. I planned well. But never meant for anyone to be aboard."

The other 'foils would arrive in mere seconds.

"If Fantomas finds out what you've done—"

"He'll kill me."

The three stood in the murmuring waters and wind. The zephyr and the sea tugged at them.

"How long?"

"It'll stop after it's over the first small bulge and then just drift with planetary rotation until it reaches the big bulge. The altitude will trigger the final sequence and it will sink."

"So we might be able to reach it on 'foils or kelpies."

The man reached up to his neck. When he spoke, his coarse voice had dropped an octave. "If not for the obvious."

Boski fidgeted. Worried at who would arrive first. To whom would the slicks show loyalty? The thought occurred to Pristina.

"Accomplices, Nilay?" Pristina unclipped the pistol at her hip, pulled it from holster, flipped the safety, and leveled it at the man.

"No," he said. His Adam's apple bobbed beneath ruined flesh.

"Last chance," she whispered.

"I act alone," he said.

She squeezed the trigger.

Among the detritus of their merriment the crew and slicks gathered, the spires listing back and forth with the living waters. Harsh whispers propagated amongst them, cliques forming along lines ideological, familial, ethical, or more esoteric in nature.

Khalid fluttered amongst the groups, arriving back at Fantomas and Pristina, guarded by Boski and the Gita-inked slick, Saed. He lingered this time. Pristina wondered at the tonal change in her voice, in Fantomas,' that caught him. Was it the sound of parents with dead children? She shook her head, fretting at both the nihilism and her failure of insight. Amr, too, had just spoken to them from *Amenaza*.

"Evar and her crew have Nilay in the spire," Khalid said. Fantomas nodded. Pristina nodded. The three lingered, looking at each other.

"Ideas?" With that word Fantomas hid his father-self. Their Captain. Tears lingered among the whiskers and oil of his beard, little microcosms of frailty better pretended to not exist.

"*Prayers from Mecca* is near: they can wait for anyone who wants to meet her. They will lose enough charge to just reach low orbit, so they lose the next drop. But the captain offered it without thought."

Fantomas nodded.

"Boski. Let everyone, including Evar's, know about this option. They need to claim 'foils and leave within five minutes," Khalid said.

Lapping waves and wind surges filled the air with lulling sounds. Words stuck in Pristina's craw, nothing fitting the needs of her heart or this moment. She thought of the girls, Cancer and Toro—

"I'm going after them. You two should accompany the crew to *Mecca*," Fantomas whispered, staring off into the undulating waters washing the isopods and prigs away.

"Shut up, stupid man. You know we're the three going," she wiped her tears. The slicks shuffled from the other two platforms onto this central one, surrounding them.

Khalid put his hand on both their shoulders and closed his eyes.

"Nilay won't make it bleeding in these waters," he observed.

"I think that was Boski's intent," Pristina said, the slicks surrounding them gazed at her with hard eyes.

"Yes it was," Boski said, rejoining them. "I told the slicks to decide as I offered the options."

"Options?" Fantomas and Khalid both

muttered.

"Options, gentlemen. They may run like bitches to *Mecca*. They may stay in the shell there with Nilay and hope for the best. Or they may come with us to rescue our fellow slicks."

"The attempt would be an honorable death. But orders are what they are and we'll not lose an entire crew to this malfeasance," Khalid said. Fantomas nodded, eyes clouded.

Boski stepped closer and lowered her voice. "Evar is scared of the waters already. She's volunteered her crew to stay with Nilay in the spire. The Mahdist in Waseem's crew all will accompany the rescue. My old crew too."

"Waseem's new," Fantomas commented.

"And quite devout. He and his cousins would be breaking their vows not to come with. Orders or not," she glanced from man to man.

"Then let's rid ourselves of these bitches and get on with it," Fantomas said. And, finally, that mad grin shone like Alpha.

The conversation with the kids had been short.

Cancer's irritation, sarcasm, and anger flavored each and every word she spoke.

All Pristina could tell the two girls was: *sit tight*. She tuned into the bridge cam and spoke to them as a mother would, forgetting the slicks nearby. Cancer faltered then, fear rendering her features dull for a moment. Toro would have none of that. *We are slicks*, she said in the tiny window in all their goggles. Everyone cheered beneath the spires and Toro smiled wide as if a private fantasy had just been fulfilled.

Amr remained serious but calm. His father told him to be careful, but to check the main hold door. *See if you can close it.*

"Listen," Khalid had said. "Listen, my son. Prepare to leave the ship by Kelpie if you can't get those doors closed. There is an observation buoy near the big bulge point *Amenaza* will reach. If you get there and the hold door remains open, abandon ship and make for the buoy. Use Kelpies. Very important, son."

So that was the best they had. Try to catch up to the ship, but if not, the kids would abandon at the end. They thought for a time to tell them to abandon as soon as it slowed. But that would be suicide. The same suicide they were undertaking with a handful of slicks.

They kept the channel open to the bridge. The three signed off to go about various duties cooked up for each, Cancer with arms crossed, Amr whispering a small *namaste*, and Toro saluting her Captain and fellow crew.

Allah, please. Pristina kept chanting in her head. *Please, Siva.*

Boski assumed control of her old crew. She stood with Waseem, their crews arrayed in a protective cresent between the three and the departing slicks. Gustavo, Nirav, and their crews. The men and one woman (she of the belly dance) slinked off, shoulders bowed, mounted their 'foils, and set off in the direction of *Mecca* without a glance back. Shamed.

Pristina turned to find Evar and her crew huddled behind her.

The woman: small, sinewy, tougher than Boski. But spooked. Her eyes gave her away. Her slicks were spooked along with her. Strange how like sought and found like. They'd been good slicks. But the deep waters and their demons proved too much for their imaginations.

"Mum," Evar said. "Captain. Mr. Sujjad. We'll go too. No bitches in this crew." Red rimmed her eyes, goggles around her neck. Mouth clenched. She glances at Boski with pure hatred.

Boski saw it too, having turned and strolled back to Pristina's side.

"Evar," Boski said. No more words followed, as if her heart knew something her mouth did not.

"I don't trust those," Fantomas said, tipping his head toward the receding 'foils and their riders. "To tell what happened here. Some of you, or all of you could go to *Mecca*. Not in dishonor. But to tell what was done. That dog—"

"Deserves nothing but the deep and its teeth," Khalid said. "But we are slicks. And vengeance is not ours to exact..." He paused uneasily, averting his eyes from Pristina and Boski. "If you will stay with him, to try and see him through to low tide... That, too, is honorable."

Evar stood nodding her head, tears flowing despite herself.

"We will see him through the bulges. And we'll tell what he's done. Justice for the slicks he—"

"Justice, yes," Pristina said, hand slapping Evar's shoulder before she pulled her into an embrace. "Get in there. Go up, all the way. That's the best bet."

Evar bowed, then turned and led her crew into

the spire.

They would not see the light of the next low tide.

Amr suspected.

He stood watching the waters pass beyond the ramp, which had cracked and lost its lower half. He thought of the Post-human drone and its warning about the AG layer. Now this. What would happen when they reached the bulges? The image of *Amenaza* reaching the first small bulge and continuing on at the same altitude filled his mind. And if this hold door remained open, waters would engulf the ship. Yet his father told him to remain on the ship until the big bulge, *then* to abandon.

It made no sense.

Ghost sharks trailed the ship in v-formations, their opaque bodies sparkling like evil promises in the dwindling morning light. In the distance Alpha drew up into the low ceiling of clouds.

"If we can close the door, we're safe," the voice startled him. When he turned, Toro stood behind him leaning for a better view.

"Let's step back a bit, eh, Miss Patton-Guererro," Amr said, his arm out between the girl and the hold door.

"The door, yes?" she continued, all nod and smile, eyes still be-goggled. Boski would chide him for having his own around his neck.

"Well, it will help. If the AG layer tracks us underwater or such. But—" Amr realized the comment unhelpful and his next unvoiced thought even worse. *There are* things *in the bigger bulges. Vast things. The biggest living things known to man or Post-human.*

"What?"

"Go get your sis so we can all talk."

"Tell me what you're thinking! She's no use. *Not* a slick." The girl put her hands on her hips and puffed up her cheeks.

"Miss, I can't be kind right now. I'm sorry. Our parents are about to murder themselves in a mad attempt to reach us. We have some decisions to make. Tell you sister that. If the two of you want to be a part of those decisions."

The child blanched, then turned red. Good. The anger might serve her.

He thought of his treatment by the other slicks.

Toro stalked away through the rows of corralled kelpies and other beasts to find Cancer. Amr took the time alone to examine the hold doors. He tested the manual mechanism and found it seized. From the school of the ship he'd had to attend before coming aboard back at Salem, he knew that unless the lock was engaged, the wheel should have some play to it. A bit more examination and he saw the door itself had been welded to the rail on which it normally slid. And, as if for good measure, the mounts for the rails were missing most of their bolts and the brackets had been torched and bent. Any pressure, even if they could get the doors closed, would burst them wide.

Amr trudged away from the hold doors and stared into the hold full of animal life. On a whim, he lay down in the water filling the hold —

understanding that despite constant circulation, animal waste permeated the brine— and floated there, eyes shut. For a time he felt weightless, without worry or concern. Then he came back to the present moment and confronted it. Options. The options were few. He did not want to play chum to all those ghost sharks. He didn't want that for his father or the girl's parents, either. There—

"What the hell are you doing?" When he opened his eyes, Cancer stood above him, her hair tied back into a sensible ponytail. She'd added a Sterling-Suit top to the bottoms (her parents would not know about the top).

"If you had the full suit, you might be able to survive in the deep, locked away from the world. A non-thing to the eaters."

"You, OK?" the younger sister asked, squatting over him.

Amr lifted himself out of the brine and muck to face the girls.

"We'll go to the bridge and watch for the first small bulge. The doors are welded open and vandalized. If the ship maintains this altitude, we abandon ship. I see there are two 'foils on the rack there. We'll take those. Might frighten the ghosts." He paused, expecting protests. Neither said anything.

"If the ship stays at surface level, then that tells us we can at least trust the ship until the big bulge apex. The question is... Do we take the 'foils out before the first bulge anyway? Our parents are coming after us. They will come through the ghost sharks we just passed through. If they can do that, then perhaps we can do it so they don't have to."

"And what then?" Cancer said.

Amr held his tongue. All the ships would be in orbit. All would be hours away from the charge needed for a rescue descent. Assuming their parents lived, assuming they found each other, they'd just be more liabilities while their parents struggled to keep all alive.

"Shite, it's a stupid idea. Just. Want to *do* something."

"The escape pod," Toro said.

"What?" Amr asked.

"The escape pod. We can get in that. It's airtight," she smiled and looked from Amr to Cancer.

"That's true, Miss, but it is not navigable in atmo. Also, not sure how much pressure it could take and it's suggested the bigger beasties are attracted by electronics, so even if it were airtight, we'd not want to go that route at the big bulge instead of abandoning. At that point, we have to leave."

"Double shite," Toro said glumly and lowered her head.

Cancer glanced at him and smiled. They pushed through the waters, Toro between them, until they reached the metal beachhead, mounted the stairs, and then clamped forward to the bridge. To watch for the first bulge.

Toro ran ahead as Amr paced beside Cancer. The big bulge loomed above the heaviest weather and might be calm compared to the other bulges. He wasn't sure about the wild life common to the summits of that mountain range of water, but maybe. Maybe they could make it that far and maybe they could get to the buoy... to that point he thought he was being realistic, but after that all he could see was certain death as they attempted to work out from the big bulge and across its diminishing siblings. And the idea that their parents might make it to the buoy was nothing but a fairy tale. It would be up to Amr to see the last two of the Guerreros to low tide and then the safety of orbit. He tried not thinking of his own father. Or of Boski and the other slicks.

Ahead, tinny shrieking echoed down the passage, then a warbled banging. Amr recognized that sound: Toro rushing down the ladder from the bridge.

She dropped to the deck as they neared the ladder. Toro raised from her crouch, small hands splayed. Amr just realized how wide and white her eyes grew when touched with awe. Or fear.

"Come on, let's see," he said to her with a pat on the back as he mounted the ladder. Cancer followed and pushed past him to stare out the forward view, silent. He peered back down the ladder and saw the child crouched there, trembling.

He turned to see what had frightened the fearless. Death loomed in the distance. A careless glance might lead one to believe a low-lying storm clotted the horizon. The first bulge. One of two small bulges. Amr tipped his head to the side. It wasn't quite mountainous. Large enough to submerge a city of Old Earth, skyscrapers and all. Not quite mountainous. But monstrous. Yes.

Behind him the ladder protested in sporadic

groans until it fell silent and Toro pushed to his side, a thin arm thrown across his lower back, her head leaning into the crook of his arm. Ahead of them, Cancer stood with her hands to the glass of the forward viewport, haloed in steam.

Amr wanted to say something heroic and encouraging. His mouth eased open, ready to give voice, but the words stuck as he scanned the bulge closer and saw vast, dark shapes swimming inside the immense wall of water. The sight awed with a sort of beauty: the waning early rays of Alpha turning the world amber beneath the pile of thunderheads, the waters a clear, cold green of deep sea, speckled in light and shadow. The titans swimming within, forms just oblique enough to never coalesce into silhouette. He meant to speak, but managed to put his arm around Toro's back, returning her hug.

5
Ghosts and Ground

This despair and weakness in a time of crisis

are mean and unworthy of you, Arjuna. How

have you fallen into a state so far from the

path to liberation? It does not become you to

yield to this weakness. Arise with a brave

heart and destroy the enemy.

—Bhagavad Gita, ch. 2 vs. 2-3

Fantomas led them into high tide, 'foil whining above the sound of storm and sea ahead.

Pristina rode Luchadora just behind him to starboard, with Khalid on the Captain's port flank. Boski trailed Pristina, and Waseem trailed Khalid, their respective crews arrayed along the outside of this formation. Fantomas, Khalid, Waseem, and both crews piloted unifoils. Pristina and Boski rode kelpies.

Pristina scanned the slicks: she didn't know

Waseem and his cousins, and noted how young they all were. Little older than Cancer, Waseem included, each shaved of head and staring in more than mortal fear at the bulges ahead, but with religious awe. She wanted to know each of them. The tall boy with beads wrapped around both wrists and tied around his neck, the shorter one with the word "Sufi" emblazoned on his pack, the two stocky slicks that were twins and the constant talkers of their crew. Waseem, with his slight frame and fastidious demeanor. Boski's crew was familiar to her, but she did not know any their names: the big one tatted up with the Gitas, his friend of the quick wit and constant smile, the other two —best friends— nearing the end of their tours as slicks at the ripe age of thirty. Boski's crew were more secular than typical Shaivist, except he of the tattooed Gitas, whereas she understood Waseem and his were devotees of the New Mahdi's Illumination.

Her headset dinged, signaling a transmission from the ship.

She heard Toro's voice. *Mama, there's* megalodons *in the little bulge.* Then ruffling and a knocking, a curse from Cancer and an admonition from Amr, followed by the sound of Toro's strings. She heard the imprecision, the shaking of her daughter's tiny hands, that signaled a quaking chest, frustration, fright. Pristina muted herself so no one would hear her, then broke formation to surge ahead of her husband.

His head flashed in her peripheral as she and Luchadora lunged past him, silent though higher than the 'foil held Fantomas.

"What are you doing?" he bellowed over the local channel. She couldn't answer and instead urged Luchadora on. Boski would remain just behind her, she knew, and both Khalid and Fantomas soon came abreast of her, the slicks maintaining their array to either side, unperturbed.

"Here we go," Khalid said over the channel, his voice a hard wedge. She didn't understand, then a wavering, blurred line insinuated itself ahead of them. The sight niggled at her reptilian brain, a yearning to match what she saw to a pattern, just out of reach. She peered at the movement. The line grew as she watched and with greater fidelity, ceased to be a line, a single thing. Out of a single whole, this line stretching with the bulge from horizon to horizon, the massive swarm emerged, and then the bodies of the individual beasts, glistening in the golden syrup of Alpha-light. Nightmares with wings and teeth and appetites.

Realization occurred, like dread.

"The good news," Fantomas said in reply. "The good news is that there are no ghost sharks in the little bulges or beyond. We make for the bulge."

And with that the bad news arrived, as they entered the swarm.

Luchadora hunkered down closer to the surface and trilled angrily, the 'foils swerving and revving, slicks steering single-handed as they leveled pistols ahead of them to clear the way. Ghost sharks made no call when shot, but flapped their ribbed wings to take them higher and away from danger, clear glistening bodies corrupted

with iron and oxygen, their wounds turning piss-
yellow. The swarm had an intelligence of sorts,
and soon it flowed around and above them,
enveloping Pristina in the sound of uncountable
wings, shallow splashes as the beasts dived into
and out of the water, and the caw and cry of the
other creatures the sharks met on their unending
tour of the planet.

A shark grazed Luchadora and would have
taken half her neck in a gaping bite, but Pristina
raised her pistol and blew away the bulk of its
head, body tumbling beneath them and knocking
her mount into a momentary lurch. They collided
with two other ghost sharks before Luchadora
righted herself and loosed a fierce bray that caused
another shark swooping toward them to alter
course. Just behind her, Boski and her mount
swerved, likewise buffeted by sharks, the hard
young woman screaming along with her kelpie's
trill— until they both fell silent.

Pristina glanced back and saw Waseem and the
crews slowing, heads turned, when he of the
Gita's exploded in an eruption of blood and
flailing limbs. The world ticked in slow motion
and the sight confounded even as the clear body
of the shark latched to his torso revealed itself
with a bite that rent the man in two. A moment
later the world sprang back into real time and
shark, body, and foil tumbled into boiling white
water corrupted with the color of raw meat.

"At my side," Pristina hissed and hauled on the
reins, pulling Luchadora into a tight loop and then
dropping herself and the beast close to the water's
surface, racing to catch up with sharks moments

before streaming past them. Luchadora jetted past Waseem and his crew on the port side of their disintegrating formation as they jerked back on their yokes to turn and follow. To her right the last three of Boski's crew circled the blood-red frenzy where Gita fell, firing into the miasma of viscera and ghosts.

Fantomas and Khalid came abreast of her, each firing up and around, taking out sharks that hovered near and looked on with bland, milky eyes and mouths that seemed to smile with mockery.

Ahead, another storm of wings grew into a column, ever turning beasts circling their prey or the carrion that remained. The slicks fell into orbit around the column of ghost sharks.

Khalid blasted at the periphery of the frenzy, first at water level, then up, one side then the other. Fantomas did the same and the other slicks, catching up, joined them, the twins protecting their rear. Pristina nodded at Gita's friend, and he maneuvered to her. With the covering fire, the two of them arced in toward the turning beasts, sliced into the circle via a gap left by spooked sharks.

A heap of gray flesh twitched at the circle's center, and atop it a small woman crouched, ready to fire on sharks that dared near. The slick with Pristina wove a ring around them as she eased alongside Boski and told her to get on behind her.

That's when she saw the sick look on the girl's face. Boski glanced down at herself, and her ship's mum saw the devastation done her arm. Only a fleshy, bleeding stump remained.

"Still thinking, mum. Not crazed a bit. I barely feel it. Can't go, though. Bleeding like a sieve. Be the death of us all. Go get your babies, mum," she said. She closed her eyes and stood very still, just lifting the pistol in her remaining hand when the slap nearly knocked her into the water.

"I *am* still your ship's mum. Get on the bloody kelpie before you *are* the death of us all," Pristina lowered an outstretched hand. Boski holstered her gun and did as told.

"What's your name?" Pristina shouted to the other slick as he led them back out the gap.

"Bhavin," he answered.

"And your friend?"

"His name was Saed," he said.

"We will hold rites for him, when we get back to orbit." On the local channel, all the but children would hear the exchange.

A pause stretched between them.

"Yes, mum," he answered. She couldn't tell if the man were angry, grieved, or both. Any of those seemed sensible.

They rejoined the formation, which broke away from the column still itself circling the dead kelpie, and headed back in the direction of the approaching bulge. The Slicks formed a perimeter around Luchadora and the two riders, a line of three 'foils leading ahead of her. The sharks despised the drone of the 'foils.

Khalid pulled alongside and sterilized and sealed Boski's stump. Last, he covered it in with a pinned-back sleeve to help keep it as clean and dry as possible.

"Swallow these," he said, holding his hand up

to Boski's mouth. She accepted the pills without complaint. "They'll give you clarity, ease you out of any shock that remains. Painkillers would not be wise under current circumstances. Better to deal with the pain but remain alert, than to be comfortable but clouded."

Boski nodded. "Of course," she said.

Khalid finished and drifted back into formation, pistol at ready.

Behind them Alpha listed beyond Ferdowsi's limb, ready to plunge behind the gas giant and casting them into premature night. Clouds loomed above, clotted masses full of flashes and rumbling. With Beta in opposition, the cloud-cover alone threatened to render them in anything like a full night. Pristina gawked at the sky and suspected night would soon arrive.

Still they pressed on through the storm of ghost sharks. A routine formed, with the whine of the 'foils keeping the bulk of the creatures at bay, while Pristina and Bhavin shot down into the water at the few clever enough to try to attack from below. The other slicks kept pegging the fliers that either lacked fear or sense to pass around these interlopers.

Static on the common channel, then a cough.

"Father. Mr. Sujjad." Amr's voice. Khalid formed part of the rear guard, so Pristina heard but did not see him.

"Yes, son," a concession. Death makes us all family, Pristina thought. No one would object at the familiar address.

"Up we go, father. I sent the girls to collect... various things. Making it an adventure for them.

For as long as they'll not understand—"

"Son—"

"But, father, I do understand. Siva, but you should see this. Vast shoals of fish like dreams drifting up between me and those shadowed swimmers deeper in. Those things are bigger than any ship I've ever seen, even a transfer orbital. Shadows shaped like great fish. I watched one of their heads turn my way, as if it saw me."

"Amr—"

"What I mean to say, father, is that we are not getting off this ship and you can't follow us just to die, slicks or no. Turn away. Get to one of the other ships. Don't be foolish."

Boski shuddered behind Pristina, crying in silence. "Stupid, brave little boy," she whispered.

"Listen to me now, Sujjad the Lesser," the term invoked indicated insult or dire seriousness. While the slicks trekked on through the sharks, shooting into the water and into the air, brine soaking them and filling their nostrils with a stinging rain, they listened to the father's voice.

"We are slicks. We do not leave our fellows behind. We do not turn. We are coming. You are not the first that we have rescued today, but you *will* be the last. In the mean time you are not just to take care of your wards, but you are to absolutely and for evermore murder this raving cowardice that has taken hold of my son. For it is his path that he should see the day when he is Sujjad the Major. No lesser intent is worthy of *my son*."

The line fell silent on this end, the echo of duplicated sounds dying, indicating that Khalid had muted his mic. The line remained silent until Amr coughed again.

"Father," the boy's voice cracked. He breathed for a moment before continuing. "Father, I have erred. I will err no more."

The line unmuted, filled with hissing echoes, and Khalid cleared his throat much like his son. "Very good, Amr. When we make orbit, we'll dine together."

"Yes, father."

All these promises of orbit, like a paradise for the sea-bound.

The rest of the conversation covered minutia that soon lost their attention. She wondered what the girls were after in other parts of the ship and if they felt frightened. She wondered at the similarities of their assurances to children and crew.

Left down, fire, middle down, fire, right down, fire. Then back. She swept the water ahead of Luchadora with bullets, adding the occasional shot straight down to their right and left and even just behind them. One of their slicks to their rear added some of his shots into the depths.

The common line grew staticky and then silent.

"They just crested the first little bulge. Which we can see now," Pristina glanced back at the man and saw him fire his weapon into the air and then point over her head. She turned and stared through the rush of ghost sharks at the approaching wall of water. Her stomach clenched and her bowels threatened mutiny.

The wall of water stood higher than the grandest city on Dar al-Salam, now reflecting the dying honey-hued Alpha light, now lit from within by lightening on the far side of the wave. The water glowed with a clear, dead green in those moments, mottled with silhouettes of an interior life discernible as darker stains against the dying flash.

They kept on, and the ghosts started to dwindle in numbers, those passing at the rear of the swarm giving wide berth: the smaller, weaker, and old. The ones most likely to be eaten by the larger monsters of the little bulge forever chasing them.

The routine continued, onward, as the sounds of the world's droning and churning threatened to hypnotize, to soften the hardness required of the next moment met.

And they kept on. The sharks became few, lone stragglers, often ailing.

Soon, Alpha no longer shone at their backs, and the cloud-cover kept out Beta's blue glow, twilight quickly deepening toward darkness as the ghosts grew sparse and the approaching bulge became a rumbling presence increasingly illuminated by variable blasts of lightening beyond the bulge or behind them. The former revealed clear silhouettes of leviathans within.

"A megalodon shoal," Pristina said on the common.

The air smelled of ozone, brine, and rotting fish churned up by the giant sine wave flowing toward them. Wind battered Pristina in fitful bursts before growing still in the lee of the wave. Lightening flashed, painting the surface of the wave in starkness so that for a moment it looked like a forty-five degree slope covered in rough glass, the tumbling thunder arriving seconds late. She blinked away the afterimage.

"This is a problem," Fantomas said.

"'Foils," Khalid said. No one knew how the larger beasts reacted to them.

"We take this task in bites. We made past the ghosts. Now we make it to the dry trough beyond," Fantomas said.

"We're sure the trough is dry," Pristina asked.

"Certain. The last three drops the cloud-cover trailed the little bulges and we zoomed in to look at the bands. All three times, dry ground."

"Ok. So we do a hundred-meter spread. Maybe the 'foils won't even attract them if spaced out enough," Pristina said. She wondered how they'd get Luchadora over the dry ground of the trough. It was not a problem she'd anticipated.

"Fair enough," Fantomas said, raising his voice to the group. "At the trough, we don't regroup, but hump straight for the second little bulge and we take the same tactic up and over it. Dry land at the second trough, then we're to the mid bulges, and the true deep."

"Regroup on the first mid-bulge slope?" Khalid asked.

"Yes," Fantomas said. Pristina felt an unsaid 'of course'. She suspected he didn't think they'd make it that far, either.

"Left flank, hundred meter spread like she said," Boski screamed to the remains of her crew, and Bhavin and the other two older slicks nodded and drifted out to port. Without any shouting, Waseem's crew rode their 'foils to starboard.

Fantomas tilted his 'foil near Luchadora, pulled his goggles up onto his forehead, and locked eyes with Pristina. They reached to each other and grasped hands for a heartbeat, then he tilted the 'foil away, pulled the goggles down, and he and Khalid steered out to port to fill in the empty spaces where Saed and Boski's 'foils would have rode.

As the formation reached its full spread, they mounted the little bulge.

A region of violent undertow and churning sucked at the kelpie and 'foils near the base until they passed the surging depression and passed onto the bulge proper. Roaring as of the greatest waterfall in all the universe smothered them for a time, until about a third of the way up the slope, the sound fell away, and a comparative silence hit with a warmer breeze.

In the distance, the whine of 'foils intensified, churning harder to make it up the forty-five degree slope. Luchadora sensed the megalodon shoal in the depths before them, hunkered low and spooked into silence, the tiny, wiry hairs on her hide standing up amid hard goose flesh. Pristina's arms prickled too, and Boski's periodic gasps made her stomach tighten even more. The lightening struck on the far side of the bulge, illuminating the interior, and Boski, leaning to one side behind her, inhaled a sharp breath and uttered a ward. Pristina, unable to look into the depths while she guided Luchadora, prepared to tell Boski to stop watching, when the young woman tensed, silent.

Looking back down the slope of water, they'd

made it about halfway up, the wave below them reflecting a final dull glow from over the far horizon. Boski gripped Pristina's arms and her eyes stretched round, mouth open. Transfixed. Pristina turned and peered down as a fortuitous lightening strike lit the waters from the far side.

The darkness below confused her for a moment, then out of the blackness features resolved. Vast, gaping mouth, the momentarily shining eyes, all rushing up toward the surface. The sense of size and utilitarian brutality paralyzed her. And then the blackness erupted from the depth, launching out into open air to starboard before dropping downward into the churning of the lower wave.

The comm squealed and Toro's voice spoke in her ear, "What is it, Amr? What?" In the background she heard the familiar sound of the child plucking at strings, nervous, followed by random stroke of bow against strings, issuing a slow, low moan. Then another moan rumbled over the comm, a deep, metallic protest. "Amr says it's the ground... the trough. It's tearing up the ship. Says if it starts to flood on little bulge two, we're leaving on kelpies. We'll update you soon."

The girl cut the line before Pristina or the others could answer. She thought Toro said 'little bulge two' but that couldn't be right. She still stared out to starboard. A numbness filled her fingers and her heart. The world tumbled beyond her reach and control, and threatened only greater violence and suffering. Still she looked to starboard.

Mist filled the space for several seconds until

she found herself staring at one of the cousins two hundred meters out. Could she really see the shock on the boy's face at this distance, or did she extrapolate only? Waseem. Waseem had taken position where now only mist and memory remained. What had they done to these poor boys? What folly did they come here to do?

Despite the nagging voice. Despite the laughter or cries of the young woman at her back. Despite the feeling of loss that tempted her to give up, to admit defeat, she opened the common and barked, "Onward. Upward. Come on, you sorry sacks of shit." and urged Luchadora to swim faster. It was all she could do to keep from diving the kelpie down into the depths to go hunting for her death.

Blue-tinged darkness fell, Shah Ferdowsi's penumbra. They crested the first bulge without further incident, and there got their first glimpse of hope. The storm thinned and Beta's blue glow seeped through, an illumination bright enough to read by. Across the valley of water before them with its narrow strip of land at the bottom, tantalizingly close at the apex of the second bulge, *Amenaza* pivoted for a moment before sinking down the far side and out of sight. The crew did not dare cheer or yell, but when she looked to either side she saw fists raised in triumph.

Along the crest of the far bulge she could see periodic patches of orange glow, mysterious and ephemeral, such that she doubted she'd seen anything more than an optical relic or afterimage.

"There she is," Fantomas growled over the

comm.

"It should have reached the bulges way ahead of us," Pristina said. "Nilay's description of its progress isn't reliable."

"Did you catch the damage at the bay doors?" Khalid asked.

"Snapped a couple still frames if you didn't," the slick, Bhavin, offered.

"I did," Fantomas said. "AGL is keeping it above water, though she's listing forward."

"If we can catch up, we could make it aboard," Khalid said.

"We'll not tally, then," the captain said.

The 'foils revved and raced downward toward the trough, while Pristina reigned-in Luchadora, surveying the dry ground below, the occasional orange glow pricking at her peripheral vision from atop that second bulge. The momentary splotches seemed... familiar.

"One after another, mum," Boski said behind her, calm again.

"The foils they can heft across, easy enough. I think we'll have to wait for the far side to catch up to us."

"I don't— oh," Boski reminded her of Toro prior to that first drop as she tried to explain the tides and bulges to her on the bridge. She smiled and turned to say something to Boski when the slick gasped, and Pristina turned to see the downward slope below them as megalodons erupted in a line roughly matching that of the 'foils they bore down upon.

"Pristina?" A question. A plea. Had Boski ever used her given name? She turned and gazed into the younger woman's eyes, leaned into Boski, clutched the back of Boski's tightly-braided head in her hand and pressed her mouth against hers, gentle, then insistent, tongue seeking and receiving reciprocation.

When she pulled away, they both were breathless.

"We keep on, Boski. Maybe we're the only hope they have," Pristina turned back to the nightmare below, though she felt calm. *Am I in shock?* she wondered. *Even if, I will use it... use it to reach them.*

The men understood their pursuit and surged toward the trough. Pristina guided Luchadora down the margin between behemoths, between paths of pursuit, smacking the kelpie's side and urging her up into a full charge down the wave-side, Boski screaming defiance.

As they descended, they watched the megalodons race after the 'foils. First down were the two older men on Boski's crew, who had maneuvered near each other on the downward slope. The joined sound of their 'foils may have been their doom. A single megalodon pursued them, surging to over-take the friends. To starboard, the twins fell next, first one, then the other as he veered in the direction of his fallen sibling, wailing. Next came the tall boy from Waseem's crew with all the beads. He was the one she'd stared at after they lost Waseem, and the closest one to fall. She saw him at the end, pulling blades from sheaths and turning on the leviathan, standing up on the 'foil and vaunting heroically into the gaping maw as it over-took him.

Fantomas, Khalid, Bhavin, and the boy with the word *Sup* on his pack reached the trough, and dry ground. Luchadora was about halfway down the bulge when Fantomas jumped from his 'foil as it spewed from the water that flowed like a tide receeding out to sea. He grabbed the craft around the central shaft and ran with it, anticipating the megalodon's gambit as it too surged from the waters and onto the washed rock of the trough. The beast after Fantomas proved the only one so driven, the other men running much like Fantomas but without further pursuit.

They passed through another zone of deafening wave-sound, and then Luchadora hit dry ground two hundred meters to starboard of the grounded shark, a ship-sized monstrosity that twisted and gaped at the kelpie riders. The two women tumbled onto the rock bed, Luchadora between them, quickly rising to their feet and clutching the beast's harness.

"Heave," Pristina yelled, and with all their strength they hauled the kelpie away from the water's edge. They collapsed against Luchadora's side and rested, their bodies again pressed close before footfalls converged and voices called to them. To rise. To keep on.

6
Sterling-suit

*"Fantomas! Fantomas has to do with this
extraordinary, this mysterious affair! Fantomas is in it!...
Fantomas!"*
-- Marcel Allain, *Messengers of Evil*
(Preserved in La Citroen DS *ships's library, Dar al-Salam Orbital
Museum & RK Cultural Heritage Preservation Society*)

With Mara's own wail, the ramp and a
section of bulkhead twice the size of
the bay door tore from the ship and
tumbled away onto the bare rocks.
Amenaza listed forward so far that Amr stared
through the gash to a surreal beach on an almost-
matching plane of gravity to the ship's own. When
the AGL functioned properly, the ship stood at a
forty-five degree angle to the sea.

Little bulge one receded in the distance, the
second soon to take them up or in. With the
gaping hole in the bulkhead stretching down
below the hold water level, brine drained through
the gash, animals behind him bleating in agitation
at the falling water level.

The lost bulkhead came to a rest, a gnarled
corner held aloft by a snippet of the AGL that
went with the wreckage, and the roaring settled to

a whistling drone of air caught in the ragged edges around the gash.

Amenaze no longer shrieked, the deck floating past the rock bed like a taunt. Occasionally they'd pass over a grinding boulder and the hull moaned in complaint.

Amr gaped at the gash where the door used to hang open.

"That doesn't look good," Cancer said behind him. She stared at the missing bulkhead, wearing —he turned to see— the Sterling-suit top and pants, Amr wanting her to be more than this spoiled and petulant girl-child. He trudged to the port bulkhead and hit the video-comm. A moment later Toro appeared on the screen.

"Bridge," she said, face too close to the camera.

"Contact the slicks. We're ripped all to hell—" He shook his head, the girl had already opened the other channel and split her attention between speaking and listening. "Toro! The bulkhead's tore away around the bay door. If we start taking on water on the next bulge, we'll have to go it on kelpies. Tell them we'll advise."

The girl nodded, already talking on the other channel. As she pulled away he saw she'd found a comfortable perch along the forward wall, where a lower shelf hung between starboard and port consoles to give the captain a better view. She'd placed one of the rough wool blankets there and beside it her instrument nestled in the case. An image flashed in his mind, of her sitting on the blanket with her knees pulled to her chest as she watched the approaching bulge.

Toro gave a thumbs up and then the screen

blanked.

He turned to Cancer.

"Can you harness one of the kelpies and bring it back here?"

"Why? What are you planning?"

"If *Amenaza* starts taking on water on the next bulge we'll be ready." He didn't understand why he had to repeat himself. She'd listened to his exchange with Toro.

She nodded but remain in front of him. He tilted his head.

"I have the whole thing," she said.

He didn't understand; begrudged the fact.

"Sterling-suit, stupid. I have the whole thing."

Oh.

"That's good. Good. You should go put the rest of it on when we're done. You'll be safer. More likely to live through this," he said. The more he thought about it, the more wise the idea felt. He nodded at Cancer, then sidled around her to go get the kelpies.

"But it's a blasphemy," she said, and when he turned her face wore the smile apparent in her voice.

"Maybe. But so is you dying out in the deep, no fault of your own. The Mahayanists say even Mara gains enlightenment. Eventually."

"I thought you were Shaivists? And so what about Mara?"

"My dad believes in God. Has a billion names, he says. I don't know. But, my point is, maybe you are wrong to wear most of a Sterling-suit. And maybe you're a little more wrong to wear all of it. But, I guess, we're all a little wrong."

He shifted and slogged away through the remains of water and waste.

"The apprentice has a brain," she said, behind him.

"Are you going to help with the kelpies?" he asked without turning.

She didn't answer, but he heard her follow, the water flowing past their ankles. A few minutes later, they had three kelpies tied to the port bulkhead just ahead of the gash, though before the video-comm. He hit the button and waited for Toro to appear.

"Bridge," she said.

"We have kelpies secured near the door. Keep an eye on the bulge and let us know when we start up. If we flood, I'll call you and expect you to hustle down here. Yes?"

"Confirmative," the girl said, a look of utter seriousness filling the screen. He laughed.

"Toro," Amr said.

"Yes?"

"Smile," and he bugged his eyes at her. The girl's own eyes widened, surprised, and she giggled before flashing a disapproving look and killing the comm.

"More hurry up and wait," Cancer muttered.

Amr nodded. This is what killed slicks. Letting the guard down during the waiting. The times between. Usually it was the drop and launch cycle: planet-side, full of activity for the slicks, and orbit, when they did more waiting than anything else. But, in essence, this was the same. They'd wait, and the moment would arrive when there would be no waiting, only action. His job was to recognize the moment. His job was to take the right action.

Up and over the second little bulge, with no problems. The AGL kept them parallel to the surface. Just after cresting the bulge, the captain hailed them and Toro replayed the transmission several times over the ship-wide comm.

We see you. We're coming, the gruff voice said amid wind and mewling kelpie.

Amr puzzled at how they caught up to the ship. He suspected *Amenaza* had lingered at the first little bulge for a time, and if so, he felt better. No way they would have survived leaving ship at that point.

It took about twenty minutes to cross each little bulge. Nearing the second trough on LB2's downward slope, Amr and Cancer grew tired of staring up the slope of water to the dark blue sky clotted with anvil-shaped thunderheads, and headed back to the bridge. The twang of the railing as they climbed up into the bridge comforted him, as did the perpetual smell of coffee infused the space. He directed Toro to send a message that they had cleared the second bulge.

"You don't have to lean into the comm like that," he said to her. Cancer snickered.

"I know. It makes people laugh, though," Toro said, switching off the comm. She turned around and walked forward to climb up on her shelf, feet dangling once she settled onto her perch. *Amenaza* neared the second trough.

Amr nodded past Toro, and she stood up on the shelf to watch, hands on glass like an echo of her big sis. *La Amenaza* hit dry ground and moaned in complaint, low vibrations growing from auditory to a tremble deep in their bones. The AGL would carry them a minuscule height lower over this trough than the last.

"Mind the con, Toro," Cancer said, tugging at Amr. Amr smiled at Toro and raised an eyebrow. The little sister did the same, but rolled her eyes, her goggles down around her neck. Amr followed Cancer.

By the time they plodded from the central access corridor and started down the stairs to the now-dry hold, stinking of dying and dead sea-things, the ship thrummed with modulation that saw them grip the railing so not to tumble to the deck. The ship turned and listed, caught and bucked. Some of this they felt, some they saw through the gash on the far side of the hold.

"The comm," Cancer said through chattering teeth, and laughed. They sprinted a drunken path through the penned kelpies, isopods, abbies, and the stilled pontoon whale.

They reached the bulkhead near their three kelpies, the beasts extending their necks to Amr, eyes full of whites as they whined at the lack of water and the ship's bucking and vibrations.

Halfway across the craggy landscape of red stone the ship groaned and creaked, snagged for a moment, bullish to break free. Amr reached out to calm the nearest kelpie when the ripping metal shriek struck him to his knees, and his hand hung in open space, the kelpies gone, the bulkhead gone, the ass-end of the ship now emptiness.

Hand extended into open air, Amr felt his

mouth hang open as if in imitation of the ruined ship. The hand balled to a fist, fell to his side. Gripping the bulkhead for support, he stood, a step from the edge and the red stone of the trough.

The cone of the ship's aft bounced over the uneven stone and came to a crumpled rest. Amr looked up, across, taking in the damage. The entire aft end had ripped away, up to the next deck, slick country, which hung above the emptiness still. The walkways leading aft had not been damaged, only the after end of the bay.

"We're still moving," Cancer said. A useful observation. Amr nodded. He shook off the paralysis. The comm hung painfully near the edge, his instinct to back away. Clutched to the rail, he unflexed his other hand and thumbed the comm.

"No more shaking," Toro said when she came on screen. "But I have all kinds of red lights on the panel. I shut off the alert again."

"Toro, we lost more of the aft hold. A lot more. Now we ride up the mid bulge. Same deal... we'll stay with *Amenaza* as long as we can. We *will* start to take on water with this much gone. Be ready to get out, yes?"

The girl's face bounced in the frame.

"Give them an update, apprentice," Amr thumbed the comm off.

"Three more kelpies. Apprentice," Cancer said to Amr. Her normally sardonic tone sinking into seriousness.

An hour up and over mid-bulge one. On the ascent, Amr killed most of the lights in the bay;

they discussed the possibility that the light might attract some of the larger fauna of the deep. This, prompted due to a paling of the entire slope of water that eventually revealed itself as the passage, beneath them, of some immense and pallid beast.

"Leviathan. They're the reason megas tend to the little bulges," Cancer said.

"And here I thought you were above the whole slick thing," Amr said.

She stared at him in return.

The other reason they killed all but the red emergency lights in the bay was so they could actually see. With the thunderheads now crowding out most of Beta's cerulean glow, they could still see if their eyes stayed accustomed, but with the light on, they spent their time blinking at after-images.

In the red glow of the bay, Amr sat with Cancer on the stairs, watching down-slope, the rippled plane stretching off to the vanishing point when he looked to either side of the ship. Scale proved difficult so close to the surface, a limited perspective, even with most of the back-end of the ship ripped away. The AGL held her a measure above the face of the waters, so the bay remained dry. Amr suspected their passage would prove uneventful from here on out. The remaining troughs would not have dry ground for Amenaza to injure herself upon, and the mega-life of the deep would hunger for much larger morsels than the slicks following in their wake. He expressed this to Cancer, wondering if it now made sense to abandon ship.

"I don't think any of us believe we'll make it

out through the trailing bulges. That buoy travels with the big bulge. Probably can be located from orbit. So maybe by the time we're there, someone has an AGL with enough charge to drop down and get us."

Amr opened his mouth to argue, then stopped. He couldn't find fault with the idea, except...

"Not sure if that's enough time for anyone's AGL to charge, though," he said.

Cancer shrugged.

Amr sighed. Just when he thought they were getting on, and she closed all up and peered at him like he was ridiculous, a child. He rose and tramped up the stairs, then aft on the walkway above the hold toward slick-country. The bulkhead where slick quarters began hung just forward of the destroyed hull so that at no point did he look down into the watery abyss. He thumbed on the comm, oil making his thumb slide against the plastic button, and leaned into the camera.

"Hello, Toro, how goes it?" he asked, turning his head this way and that. The girl laughed.

"You stole my trick," she said.

"Hey, mum, do you know how to open a channel to the transfer orbital?"

"I've seen da— The Captain, hail them. So, yep, I can do that," she said.

"Ok. I think we're about four hours from the buoy. Hail them and ask if they can get word out to the other ships. To see if someone has charge enough to drop down and get us at that point. Maybe five hours, enough that the others make the buoy too."

The girl smiled wide and offered another *confirmative* before closing the channel.

Lost a moment in his thoughts, Amr detected movement directly below him in the bay, near the wrecked edge. All the pens lay well forward of this. He scrabbled to the edge and glanced over. Cancer hunkered on the deck, peering outward.

"What do you—"

She gestured up with an outstretched palm. He raced forward along the walkway, and then turned and descended the stairs in three great swings down the rails, his full-out sprint collapsing to a jog as he neared Cancer and the precipice. He huddled beside her, leering out at the vastness. At the first mid-bulge apex, the thunderheads loomed like canyon walls, the blue light of Beta spilling down to bathe the sea in deathly shades. Farther out, between tendrils of low clouds and mist, the two little bulges sprawled, half as tall as the mid-bulge. The stone of the last trough glistened like a stone river in a valley of water, the first trough obstructed by LB2. Lightening cascaded in the canyon above and the scene trembled with starkness, marring his vision.

"Look," Cancer said, pointing. And he saw, the slicks, some of them at least, trudging across the river of stone.

"The crew. I see."

"No, stupid, look closer," she said.

He turned to her instead, waiting for her to acknowledge his irritation. She glanced at him and raised her voice, "*Look!* Before we're too far over and you can't see!" He shook his head and chewed at his cheek as he squinted down again.

River of stone, slopes of water lit by the occasional flash of lightening and by the now constant glow from Beta. A darkness there behind the crew. What—

"Oh, Siva, they have a mega on them."

"That's one thing. It's grounded, yes? But look behind that. Look!"

The ship was starting to tilt for the downward journey over MB1. Just before the scene slid out of view, he saw it: the orange glow, in single nodes and groups, arranged in a vector angled toward the slicks who traversed the stone. Something, or some number of things, angled toward them. Something aware of the slicks. Something coming for them, unafraid of the mega that stood in the way.

They sprinted back up to the bridge and Cancer opened the comm. Toro sat on the ledge directly behind them, stroking a new tune to life that started sure, grew, wavered, and died with a yelp of the strings, only to start again and proceed a bit further.

"Will you please stop that?" Cancer said, turning from the comm.

"No."

Amr rubbed his forehead and closed his eyes.

"We don't have time to talk, Cancer," her mother said over the comm.

"There's something after you. We saw it from the top of the bulge—"

"Yes. Thanks. We know," her mother's answered. "Out."

"Typical," Cancer hit the console.

He knew he shouldn't but the words flowed

before his brain could intervene. "Did you mention that we saw something other than the mega?"

She punched the console again, then turned and pushed past him and trundled down the ladder. Her footfalls against the metal grate diminished as she retreated toward the bay.

"Wanna hear a song of old earth? It's called 'Cry Baby Cry'. Cancer always reminds me of it."

Amr stared at Toro, rubbing his temples. Headache coming on. Stress did it to him, he was coming to understand. He scoffed; shook his head.

"You can be a meanie," he said.

Toro shrugged, and set her bow to strings, beginning the song regardless. Amr sighed but waited out the tune, a short, simple ditty. When finished, she bowed, bow in one hand, violin in the other. He clapped and told her "very good."

"I'm going to check on her," he said.

Toro nodded, eyes cast downward, shoulders slumped. "I'm all alone," she said.

"Why do you say that? Your sis and I are both here with you. And our parents and fellow slicks come for us."

Her eyes lifted to him. "Ok," she said.

"It will be. I promise," he stepped to her and patted her back. Before he knew it, she'd stood on the ledge and wrapped her hands around his neck in a strong hug. Her thin frame trembled.

"Why the worry, now, miss bravery herself?" he grabbed her arms and guided her to sit. Her face was flushed and tears tumbled silent from her eyes.

"I made a song for the megalodons, but not for the bigger things in the deep."

Amr shook his head, brow furrowed. Toro exhaled in frustration.

"It kept us safe. I don't know if I can keep us safe now, here, in the deepest sea."

Amr knew such childishness would only earn ridicule among slicks, even as they held on to their own superstitions and folk wisdom. He saw no reason to tear away the magic of this power she believed her songs possessed.

"But you're wrong," he said. Her mouth gaped and she searched his face, probably for traces of mockery. "You have a song. A new song for the deep. The one you were working on when Cancer hailed the slicks."

"But that's nothing," Toro said.

"It's not. It's the one that sees us through. Yes? Don't give up now. You'll need to finish it before we reach the big bulge apex. All the greater beasts of the deep will sense the... reverberations against the hull and tremble away from such a mystery as this."

They both grinned. Amr felt a glassiness in his eyes that he blinked away. He stood and patted her on the back again, squinting against the orange glow in the trough they descended toward. His smile faltered.

It wasn't until twenty minutes later, as they neared the first mid-bulge trough, that the glow resolved into individual beings, diminutive by human standards, but otherwise humanoid in form. Sliding down and into the trough, it became clear *Amenaza* would pass directly through a mass of the creatures.

"I'll be back," Amr said and slid down the ladder, and bolted aft.

In the bay, Cancer stood ankle-deep in water near the ledge, a pistol in hand. The kelpies against the wall had calmed with the rising water, though it didn't reach the other kelpies and abbies still sprawled on the dry deck around the dead pontoon whale.

Amr came alongside her, gun still holstered, but ready.

"They're floating past, but underneath us, too, looking up."

He saw what she described, the faces peeking up to them, some with detached expressions, others smiling with needle-toothed mirth. Eyes stared, deepest black or reflective it was hard to say. Others beckoned, long arms wafted as if in greeting or farewell. Out there in the azure-dark a murmur filled the breeze, *mermen calling each to each,* Amr thought, an echo of one of his father's strange sayings from a past lost to history and Post-humanity. They sounded like children in distress, mewling babies or playground tikes warring against a bully, or being bullied. In their cries and exclamations, the wide range of human emotion found stunted imitation. Laughter and cries mingled, rose, and fell away.

Amr raised his pistol toward a particular swimmer at the surface who kicked effortlessly to within arm's distance of the now-submerged ledge. The creature stopped kicking and looked into Amr's eyes, tilting its head before pulling the fish it clutched out of the water and taking a bloody bite from its flank. It watched them, face corrupted with blood and gristle, until obscured by distance.

In this manner, they traveled across the mid-bulge trough.

What seemed an eternity later, without a shot fired or an attempt to board made, they passed from the trough and started up the second mid-bulge. The water had edged closer to the pinned animals. Amr pushed his ankles through it and hit the comm.

"Call them, Toro, tell them 'mermen ahead'... don't let them close the channel without telling them. And, Toro?"

"Yes, Amr?"

"When you're done, just leave the channel open." She nodded and instead of the screen blanking, it remained on while she hailed the others. On her end it would hold a single blank square since none of the trailing slicks were outfitted to provide a video feed, and several other lit squares showing the other comm locations throughout the ship. Each of those would now show her face, talking to the slicks.

Walking away, he listened to the exchange.

"*Amenaza* to field crew," Toro's voice.

"Toro—" the ship mistress answered.

"Mermen ahead, Momma. There's mermen all over the trough."

Silence filled the line, then static and a burring sound in the distance.

"We know. We're coming," her mother's voice rang over the comm, strained, and then the connection died.

"Keep it open, Toro," Amr hollered. He heard a tinny "aye" in reply. If the slicks hailed, Toro would be there, waiting in her goggles, sitting on her shelf. If Cancer and he were close enough to a comm, Toro would hear them, and in turn—

"Oh, Siva," Cancer said as Toro's new song floated from all corners of the ship.

"Shut up, you stupid abbie," Amr said.

Cancer stalked from the edge and leaned into his face when she neared him, about to tell him— but he cut her off.

"No. No. I mean it. Shut up. Your sister is up there and feels... alone. Alone and you haven't comforted her once. Not once have reached out to her to let her know... I don't know... that she's not alone. She's a child. Shouldn't be in training yet. Her violin is like that Sterling Suit of your."

"And what is that supposed to mean?"

"Oh, come on. You wear it to protect yourself from being something you despise. From being like *us*. Without it you don't feel in control. She plays her songs for the same reason. Deal with it."

Cancer stood with her hands on her hips, nose crinkled, lips tight, until a harsh smile unfurled and a twinkle lit her dark eyes. She turned and sprinted through the water to the comm near the gash, the kelpies yelping at her in surprise. Hitting the button twice —the comm window would flash on the bridge, drawing Toro's attention—Cancer leaned into the camera.

"Shut up, you stupid little abbie," Cancer said in imitation of Amr, turned and grinned at him, then back to the comm. "Shut up your stupid, insipid screeching that nobodies likes. It drives me crazy and it drives everyone crazy, you spoiled little brat." Cancer choked with giggles and tumbled against the wall, shrill laughter echoing in the hold.

Amr strode to her and before he realized it, he kicked Cancer in the hip with his steel-toed boot. Hard. She yelped, then fell silent, clutching her side, the pain collapsing and whitening her face.

He felt unreal, like he stood in a dream. He'd never struck anyone before. Never lashed out in anger. Even blasting the Post-human had not rocked him quite like this. Leaning his face into the comm he called, *Toro!*

The camera showed her sitting on the ledge, wracked with sobs. Ever attentive, she scooted off the shelf and stepped to the comm, her flushed, tear-streaked face coming into full resolution.

"Apprentice, you will *not* stop playing and that is an order. Do you understand me?"

"But—"

"No. She is no slick," he said, repeating her own words. It occurred to him, how strange a habit they had, repeating the detritus of past conversations to each other. Little flotsam bits of found wisdom. "Only you and I, here, and slicks do not give in to despair and fear. You will keep playing and that is that. Yes?" More flotsam, to keep her afloat. Maybe to keep him afloat as well.

Her face bubbled for a second with a last sob, but she wiped the snot from her nose and nodded, the hurt finally resolving into something else. Defiance, he thought. *Good.* He gave her a smile and a thumbs-up before stepping away from the screen.

"You," Cancer said, eyes narrowed, standing in a crouch as if ready to attack.

He wagged a finger at her and walked through the pens toward the stairs, where he stopped. The water was closer. The ship would soon be at the second mid-bulge apex. Then one more trough and the final ascent. He reckoned the AGL's rate of decline sufficient to see them through.

Cancer strode to him, taking time to deliver several punches to his mid-section that he simply ignored until it seemed she'd set to him with her nails, and he grabbed her wrists and shoved her toward the stairwell. She trotted up and then faltered for a moment, apparently unsure where to go. After hesitating, she turned and headed aft toward slick country, where she disappeared into the warren of crew quarters and facilities.

Amr did not want to gaze back out to watery slope behind them, but he must. He needed to confirm something he was unable to earlier, amid the orange glow of the mermen, to discern if it was real or imagined.

He moseyed back down into the water, gingerly stepping to the edge where the sea lapped at his legs above the ankles. Down-slope, he stared, squinting his eyes. The canyon of thunderheads still gaped above, and the world shone in shades of black, navy, cerulean, aqua. Glints of orange here and there. The first mid-bulge stood opposite them, blocking out the little bulges, so that sky and sea mimicked each other with their own strange canyons. Down-slope, and he finally confirmed what he thought he'd spied earlier.

Trailing them, almost far enough into the briny mist and darkness to merge with the azure-dark sheen of starlight upon the choppy sea, a wake followed in their path. Below the foamy brine of that wake, a vast outline stood in relief against a slight but discernible orange glow.

7

A Requiem for Mermen

There goes my soldier girl
she's so far away...
—The Polyphonic Spree, "Soldier Girl"
(From the Dar al-Salam Pre-Spike Earth Library; United States of Texas
Popular Heritage Collection)

The slick, Bhavin, would not attend rites for Saed once they reached orbit. Pristina's heart attenuated in the gravity well of that broken promise.

At the first trough, she and Boski tried in vain to drag Luchadora across the craggy ground, and finally resolved to await the approaching bulge. But in their efforts, they attracted the attention of the grounded megalodon.

The creature turned its barnacle-encrusted head to and fro, mouth gaped wide and gills splayed, sucking at the air. A series of lacerations covered the head in a loose grid, as if it recently caught itself in some vast net. The entire body, only slightly smaller than *Amenaza's* main bay, flexed back and forth and Pristina wondered if the beast did itself harm under its own tremendous weight. A stench of kelp and rotted fish wafted from the mouth as it heaved and silently bellowed.

The moment after the bulge overtook Pristina, Boski, and their mount, the great shark, too, would thrust up into the wall of water and come for them. Teeth oblique and serrated in that stinking maw dreamed of sweet union with their flesh. Behind those teeth, ribbed gaps lined the shark's mouth and throat, where it might store food for later consumption.

In the end, are we only bits of meat to greater beasts? Pristina shook her head, face composed. *My babies. My girls.* The voice refused censure.

Khalid and Fantomas altered course to come to their aid, and she screamed at them. *Go get our children!* The two men, broken by their own strength, turned and walked across the red stone, mounting the second little bulge minutes in advance, along with Bhavin and the Mahdist boy, whom she still only knew as "Sufi."

When the waters came, Boski and she were ready, launching Luchadora into the wave and then grappling back into the saddle.

Thirty seconds into the second bulge, Luchadora streaking upward at amazing speed, Pristina sensed the bulk of the great shark thrashing to gain purchase in the waters flowing down upon it. From above, a familiar whine surged near and Bhavin descended past them, eyes dark and clear, a quick salute offered, then he surged to the shark and along it's flank as it ungrounded itself. He passed close to the beast's creamy-black eye, pistol held horizontally and fired one, two, three, and a fourth time. The Black eye hemorrhaged piss-yellow.

He angled the 'foil downward and away, riding in the leading shallows of the bulge and drawing the attention of the mega, for a time.

Truth be told, Bhavin could still be out there, riding the interstice between ground and sea, drawing the attention of deadly sea-things, mocking them with his sardonic grin and flippant demeanor. A Desi myth, a thing to tell children at bedtime. *He laughs with Siva and all the gods in the shallows between the red rocks and the deeps of the bulge, taunting the would-be predators of this world of rended flesh.* The story would elicit a song from Toro and she'd find some elaborate and mighty title befitting the man or the myth of the man.

Luchadora took them up and up, eventually joining the 'foils that labored up the slope. They'd neglected to spread out this time, and the upward slog proved slow and nerve-wracking.

Mounting the crest, the first mid-bulge loomed across the next trough like a vast canyon wall in the cerulean night. They picked up speed on the race down, and neared the trough when a torrential downpour hit them. It felt like the bulge falling upon them, and an elemental fear shook Pristina, causing her to turn and look upslope. The wall of water churned and frothed above them, and a pattern emerged from a confluence of watery vectors. The pattern, black lines against pale, cross-hatched. Like a net.

Siva.

The mega re-emerged behind them, bursting from the wall of water just as the uncanny valley lightened under parting thunderheads. The mega cascaded upon them, casting hungry shadows, as they spilled from the receding water and then washed away in the surge the shark sent chasing them.

Khalid and Fantomas tumbled together as Sufi sprawled to their side, one hand clutching his 'foil. The three men spun in the dying waters. Luchadora thrashed her tail in the surge and pushed her riders past the downed 'foil riders before stalling on dry stone.

Then the waters receded, and Pristina rolled from the saddle in momentary exhaustion. On her back, she stared up at the mega, it's mouth like small ship's bay, the conical mass tipping toward one morsel then the next, in vain. How easy it would be to stand, and bolt the short distance, and cast herself upon the oblique teeth.

Instead she rolled over and onto her knees, peering up at the next beast in their way. The mid-bulge.

In the night-glow, the slicks breathed for precious moments in tired, crouched poses. She'd been in the water too long and the oils on her skin were starting to break down, her fingers pruning up, body chafing. Mist filled the air, either drizzling rain or an eternal haze between bulges.

Both the mega and Luchadora grounded, Pristina didn't see how they could do anything but repeat their last movement, this time without Bhavin's distraction.

Giving up seemed reasonable. *If anyone reaches orbit, will you hold rites for me?* The slick in her screamed, an image of Cancer and Toro held like a mental talisman, a wordless mantra. Outward her face remained placid, though her hands trembled and her legs felt weak, standing up after so long in the saddle.

She prepared to send Boski along with Sufi: both small of frame, the unifoil should manage. But the three men sprinted to Luchadora, 'foils neatly wedged atop their shoulders, and threaded their belts around the kelpie's harness as handholds. Boski saw what they were doing, and secured her own belt at the side of the saddle, motioning for Pristina to do the same on the other side. And like this, they traversed the second trough, Luchadora in tow.

Cancer hailed them about the mega as they trekked across, and Pristina acknowledged the fact, but didn't have time or energy to talk. For some reason —perhaps the mid-bulge was simply too large or more mist filled the air— they could barely discern the ship as it pivoted over the top of the bulge.

Reaching the first mid-bulge, they started up with wary glances at the mega. Perhaps with enough distance it would lose interest, Fantomas suggested, but Pristina knew that one of their number would need to draw the beast away and even that would just mean a temporary respite from its pursuit.

"One well-placed charge and we'd be done with the thing," Fantomas said uselessly. They carried no ordinance beyond their pistols.

The mega's tail fin thrashed audibly as it returned to the sea, and pursuit. No one spoke.

The opening in the clouds lingered, bleaching everything in stark shades of cobalt and beryl, a spectrum of blue punctuated at either end by dark shadows and shining foam. An umber glow, burning at times as warm as firelight in the distance, though that could not be right, seemed to flow toward and then around the megalodon, until its mouth gaped and glowed in its submarine path toward them. It looked like Mara's own creature, lit from within by the flames of the Avici hells. As its jaws smothered the light, the beast dove and left them, apparently uninterested in the dwindling morsels they represented.

Pristina slowed Luchadora, looking at her husband, the first mate, and the remaining slick besides Boski.

"And what just happened?" she asked.

"Good fortune," the boy suggested. Pristina felt Boski cough in derision behind her.

"Whatever. Onward. We near *Amenaza* and the children," Fantomas said. Khalid nodded, and they returned to their previous pace.

"How long will the 'foils run on their charge?" Pristina asked Khalid, filling the wind-whipped moments with talk. Distraction.

"Long enough, mistress," he answered over the comm as they returned to their hundred-meter spread.

An hour up and over.

As they crested the first mid-bulge, they saw *Amenaza* passing through the trough amid a clot of the same umber glow that had overtaken the mega.

They took the downward slope at full speed, dialing up the magnification on their goggles to see the ship passing amid the glow.

"Mermen," Fantomas said over the commons. The wind and water smelled brackish. Pristina shivered.

It took time before they could make out details, but the ship seemed to pass from the trough without issue, though they soon realized they'd made a tactical error in believing they stared upon an isolated gathering of the indigenes.

Surrounding them, the creatures swam, initially invisible in the surges and ripples of the downward slope, but once sighted, the umber-to-orange glowed deep in their bones to set their frames alight. Like so many simple dangers, they were beautiful. A lie of nature, this beauty.

Maybe all beauty... She thought of Toro's grin, her silly games of pretend. She thought of Cancer, before this senseless hatred marred her. The smart, funny child full mirth and potential.

No. My girls are beautiful.

As they reached the trough, the 'foils angled in to join the lone kelpie. Watching their progress, Pristina realized an ardent procession of mermen followed each 'foil, whereas only the occasional swimmer kept pace with Luchadora. "Sufi" had it worst of all, the creatures veering in near him and reaching out as though he were holy, touching and stroking him. The boy's eyes, wide and white, reflected the starlight, and he occasionally yelped when one of the mermen pricked him with a barbed thumb or chitinous back-hand.

"Mi ho," Pristina called, but the boy, new to the crew, did not understand her.

"Slick," Boski yelled, and caught his attention.

He looked from her to Pristina.

"Mi ho, come here, now," Pristina said.

"Aye," he said over the common, and angled toward Luchadora just as another barb caught his ankles, a gripping hand sliding away into the waters. When he drew alongside them, Boski already understood what was to be, lashing her remaining hand in the belt she'd left on the saddle.

"Turn it away from the kelpie before you leap," Boskie nodded at the 'foil. "Grab my pack and hold on. You'll have to ride bareback behind me."

"I—"

"You *nothing*. Act like a slick and take the order, son," Boski said. Pristina stifled a smile. She felt the extra weight burden Luchadora as the 'foil tipped and then tumbled away, the drone murdered in the fall.

"Foolish," Fantomas said over the common.

"The creatures were about to take him down, and we'd have lost the 'foil anyway," Pristina said.

"Doesn't matter. It's done," Khalid said.

Khalid and Fantomas led an entourage of mermen, apparently driven to hostility by the whine of the unifoils. Each man was large enough that only a few dared near, and those met lead in response. They passed from the trough and started up the last mid-bulge, mermen still in tow behind Fantomas and Khalid, Luchadora swimming undisturbed, if fatigued. *See us to these children and you'll need never labor again, good girl.* Pristina thought, patting the kelpie's mane.

Pristina rested her eyes on the trip up, except midway when she heard the boy whisper *My lord*.

Look. to Boski. Boski laughed a moment later. Pristina opened her eyes to see what they were on about, and saw the spire whale pods drifting up the mid-bulge all along the slope, cities from some dark fairy tale afloat in the sea. She stole herself to consider that, in fact, some of them just might cities, thinking of the spire Boski and she had explored, where the traitor Nilay and Evar and crew might still ride. Maybe they rode in one of these spires and even now stared out at their comrades trekking across the surface of the deep.

A poetic conceit. The voice laughed. Those slicks were dead.

She closed her eyes again, and only opened them when Amr's voice broke the night's calm. The slicks were soon to crest the bulge and would be able to lock down again on *Amenaza*. To see her, to know that she was safe for awhile longer.

Amr opened the channel, but he spoke to the girls.

"Toro, brace for impact. Cancer, get out here *now.*" Then he must have stepped from the comm, because she heard no more at that point. The feed from the bridge remained open, and she called that up in the goggles with practiced eye-gestures and blinks, only to see Toro jump from the ledge along the forward ports and run out of the frame.

"Hello, Amr? *Amenaza?*" Fantomas said.

They crested the mid-bulge, the trough glowing below them like a molten river, obscured now by mist, now clearly filled with an assembly of mermen, and above them the big bulge hung, so vast it felt like stumbling upon the raiment of a god, or the limb of a planet left here by accident.

Sea sounds echoed and warped in the odd seascape. While the others gaped, Pristina peered down through a gap in the mist at the dark sliver of *Amenaza* as she passed into the bulk of mermen in the trough.

And she then she saw it.

"No," she said. The common band remained open and the other's looked at her. "No."

She heard Khalid's sharp intake of breath as he saw the shadow. Fantomas bellowed into the night, his voice lost in a space so full of sound it could not abide him his voice.

The mega's silhouette wavered against an orange glow, as if swimming an electric sea, and accelerated toward the ship.

Mermen tried to board the ship as *Amenaza* passed through the great assembly. The chattering sounds of the multitude raised the hairs at the base of his neck. An extra pistol in hand, Amr stood at the edge and shot merman after merman. A stronger man would not think it, but they seemed as human as any slick. As sentient as the post human he'd shot... a few drops back. It stole something from him, each time one of them tumbled with a grunt into the waters. He'd fulfill his duty, but damn it, it be nice if *she* would get over herself and help him. Cancer had not emerged from slick country nor answered any of his pages over the comm.

When he ran out of ammunition, he planned on using his blades. It meant close combat. Close combat meant the merman that came aboard after he fired his last shot would be the one to kill him.

And he had more fingers than shots left to fire.

But he would do his duty.

The water almost filled the bay back to the stairs and reached his knees when he stood near the ledge. A misty rain hit his face when the wind shifted. The three kelpies tied nearby huffed in pleasure at the mist. If *Amenaza* made it past the mermen, he'd gather the girls down here and they'd wait out the two-hour trip up, then leave for the buoy. He worried now if it would be easy to find or if they'd get there and find only the summit of a featureless sea.

In attentive reverie, he saw the wake rise up from the sea and resolve itself into a blackness under the cerulean radiance that leaked through the clouds. A crack formed in that blackness, and then expanded into a tunnel of light. It made no sense, but as it sped to reach the ship realization dawned and Amr recognized the teeth and the shape of the snout, the dorsal fin towering in the night. The glow inside the mega confounded him, until it grew closer still and it became clear: the mermen riding upon the palate and within the bulbous flaps around the mouth, as well as upon and around the mega, bodies trailing from lines lashed around the conical head.

Dumbstruck, he stared upon this sight for longer —he would later conclude in self-condemnation— than he should have. It loomed large enough to be another ship performing a docking maneuver in orbit. Behind it, in contrast to the dark bulk, the molten river of mermen filled the trough, and behind that, the misty gloom of the last mid-bulge, where the slicks would now descend and attempt to follow. Amr shook his head, but if anyone could make it, Fantomas and his father were the slicks. And they had Boski, the hardest woman he'd ever met. Well, in a way. In another way, Cancer had everyone beat.

The megalodon dipped into the waters, and then rose with speed, barreling toward the ship. Amr snapped out of his distraction and splashed to the comm. He told Toro to brace for impact and for Cancer to get out here. Then he turned and looked outward, the shark moments away. He ran.

He reached the stairs, took two steps at a time to reach the top, and no impact. A moment's hesitation, and he sprinted aft to find Cancer. He knew where Toro waited. He busted through portal to slick quarters, past bunks and the head, then into the commons. Cancer sat at the steel table where the slicks played cards between drops, the Sterling-suit on the floor. A linen tee-shirt and shorts still clung to her svelte body.

Amr lurched in the portal and she turned to him, eyes red.

"I," she said. She never finished the thought. And later — following what would happen to her at the station she'd later name after this cursed ship— he would wonder. If she'd been able to complete her thought, maybe peace would have embraced her on the other side of that utterance. The admission or confession, whatever might have been on her lips.

Instead, the ship jarred and Amr went sprawling, biting his tongue and bashing his skull against the bulkhead.

"What—"

"Just, come on," he didn't know how to explain. He did have a plan. They'd run forward and get Toro, come back to the door at slick country and use a fire hose from the nearby fire station to lower down over the back of the beast (he felt certain it would gorge itself on the pontoon whale and other penned animals) to where their kelpies hopefully still waited, unharmed.

A wistful glance at the Sterling-suit, he grabbed her hand and led her at a run from slick country to go get her little sis. When they opened the door to the main bay, he stepped out and saw his plans crumble. It was the last time he'd face little Toro. They would leave her. They would climb down on the back of the beast and leave the little girl to this nightmare. Because they all died otherwise.

He saw all this clearly in that crystal moment, eyes locked with Toro. Her goggles on, he could not see her eyes, but he saw she understood.

Amr yelled to her...

Toro loved Amr. Not in some foolish little-girl infatuation. No. She didn't want to talk about him with other girls back at school in Dar al-Salam, and giggle. She loved him. Like... like a brother, she supposed, though she'd never had such a thing. In contrast to Cancer, a brother might be nice. A bigger person, but still a kid in all the ways that mattered, who would take up for her and play with her. Who was interested in her and what she said and the things she did. Her songs, her ideas. Who looked at her with smiling eyes, and saw something good. This is what Amr had become over seven short drops and their extended travels upon the seas of Shanama.

Bow pressed to strings, she teased out the last movements of the new song. She'd almost finished it, thanks to Amr. For a time she'd considered giving up, but that would let him down. She leaned against the console, sitting on her ledge, and gazed out past the mermen in the water, who stared back at *Amenaza's* passage, enraptured by her song. Her eyes grew hard, a slick's death-stare. The bulge loomed ahead, wall-like. If the little bulges could swallow the great mosques in Dar al-Salam, and the mid-bulges were twice their height, the big bulge loomed as tall as the mountain range that bisected Salem's fertile crescent from Golly. These were the closest approximations her young mind could fathom.

Her hand ceased in mid-stroke and she pushed up from the comfy position to stand upon the console, feet wide, bow held high and ready to descend, to finish the song, to see them to the big bulge and away from their last danger in these merfolk.

She tucked the bow carefully in the crook of her arm and then reached up and pulled the goggles back into place on her eyes, adjusting them. Perfect. An evil grin played upon her lips, as she held the bow above her head again, surveying her audience through glass. The bow descended in silence and remained docile against the strings, seemingly aware of its potency.

To and fro, the tone gentle, but sure. This song whispered of slicks, of strength, of love. It did not compromise or allow for doubt, growing strident and sharp, but not angry, and never out of control. It rose, because hope and strength increase, even in the face of the deep. Across megalodons and ghost sharks, broken AGLs and hateful siblings, traitors and mermen, leviathans and bulges great and small. The song suggested it all; the song defied it all.

The goggles contained her tears even as her mouth trembled amid its smile. It almost escaped her, the comm, Amr's voice. Her arm faltered and the song died. *Brace for impact?* Her head tilted at the mermen down there.

The song had worked! They swam away in fear.

She beamed, triumphant.

Toro shook her head, placed her bow and violin at her feet, and then jumped from the ledge to go tell Amr he was wrong, that they were safe now. That she'd done it. *The song did it.*

As she descended the rackety ladder in three jubilant bounds, she heard her father's voice. *Daddy!* He'd be proud of her. First, Amr, then she'd come back and hail the slicks. Or she might need to go down to the bay and play the song to the mermen at *Amenaza's* rear, to remind them their place as the other slicks passed through the great assembly.

These thoughts filled her head as she chugged headlong down the central corridor, stamping out a staccato rhythm on the steel mesh. The ship shifted and sent her tumbling against bulkhead and then deck with a grunt.

Brace for impact. What could have hit the

Amenaza, though? The central corridor descended as it ran aft, and more drastically just prior to the main bay, so that as she peered down the walkway, listening to an odd clicking, multiplied into a dozen sources, interspersed with the mewling of abbies and kelpie yelps. Another sound, below these, played bass. A rumbling, jarring, background tremor that set her teeth to chatter. Toro stood, checking her legs and arms, but no harm done.

She sprinted the rest of the distance to the main bay.

The sight, when she stumbled to a stop within the corridor, proved so unreal she felt not fear or awe, incredulity or despair. A mega sprawled below, filling the bulk of the main bay, thrashing side to side and catching the penned beasts in great lurching bites on one side, then the next. The beast was so large, it reared up and tore away the walkways leading aft over the bay toward slick country.

That's when she saw Amr standing ahead of Cancer, on the far side of the damaged walkway, straight aft from Toro. Walkway gone, mega positioned to devour anyone attempting to descend the stairs down into the bay, and now they came, the dozens upon dozens of mermen, flesh less orange up close than amber with veins of red visible beneath. Eyes large and black, arms and legs barbed, heads hairless, ears nonexistent, mouths wide and filled with needled teeth, the flesh itself mottled with patterns both natural and tattooed.

She couldn't reach Amr. He couldn't reach her.

She stared at him. *I am a slick*, she thought. *I will not fear, I will not despair.* Toro nodded at him, telling him it was okay. Get her sister out. *I am a slick.*

"Toro, the escape pod," Amr yelled. "The escape pod!"

Toro turned and ran.

The slicks on the water witnessed the video feed from the ship that would eventually be used to conclude Pristina's study, *On The Demise of Captain Fantomas Patton-Guererro & Loss of La Amenaza Elegente.*

Full into the mass of mermen, the entire trough alight as with watery flames, Khalid's 'foil was ripped from under him by a massive merman, and the man sent flying forward into water and foam. Pristina hauled Luchadora into a hard left and the kelpie strained below the surface, all three riders in tow, where she jostled and bit the merman pulling Khalid under and the first mate clutched at one of the belts still lashed to the saddle. Luchadora surfaced, and then kept pace under the added weight, nipping at mermen who strayed too near, the four slicks, three on her back and one holding head above water to the side, holding guns at ready. Pristina doubted any of the guns remained loaded.

Fantomas still trailed, still amassed, mermen, angry at the 'foil drone.

In the corner of her eye, Pristina saw movement. The bridge feed. She maximized it with a careful blink, and saw Toro stumble to the ledge and grab her instrument. The girl turned at a sound, and climbed up on the ledge, obviously frightened.

"Please, no," Pristina whispered.

The child stood, instrument in hand, staring to the side, where Pristina understood the ladder was located. The bridge filled in moments with the piss-yellow creatures, who stood and regarded the child instead of attacking. An odd moment: a meeting between worlds. Toro realized herself, and stared directly into the comm, over the heads of the mermen.

"A requiem for mermen," she said, voice cracking, unaware of any irony the title held. She pronounced "requiem" as *reckwim*, a word she'd seen on sheet music, but had perhaps never spoken.

She lowered bow to strings and played the song. A song she'd never heard Toro play before. A beautiful song; a strong song. A song befitting a slick such as her. It played even after the comm camera could not see her, crowded out by the mermen filling the bridge. It played from fingers so young, so brave, until it died in a tumble and crash along with all the universe that lived in her mother's heart.

"I have Cancer. We're leaving on kelpies. We'll see anyone else that makes it at the buoy." Amr's voice, only. He could barely speak.

Fantomas stilled. His baby. His little slick. He hurt so deep in his bones he couldn't yell or cry. It would be an insult, a distraction from the loss. These things, these monsters clawed at him, angered at the 'foil's drone. He looked over at the kelpie and the slicks it played savior to. No mermen dogged it. He understood, and it was enough at this point. It was right.

Voice full of phlegm, he stared at his wife across the distance. At Khalid.

"Go get our children," he said, and pulled away, turning back toward the river of flame. He heard his wife's scream, her anger.

No.

But it was the only way.

Fantomas Patton-Guerrero's last words, hissed over the comm before the 'foil he rode shrieked, skittered free from the water, and then died, rang in the other slick's ears, *Come on, you bastards, I'll show you how a slick dies.*

The words would conclude, with a final fade to black, the study compiled from Pristina's recordings.

8
The Last Slick

I'm happy for to see ye home, hurroo, hurroo

I'm happy for to see ye home, hurroo, hurroo

I'm happy for to see ye home

All from the moon of Shanama

So low in flesh, so high in bone

Oh Captain we hardly knew ye.

—Traditional

The buoy found them. As Amr and Cancer neared the bulge apex, the buoy sensed their local channel and signaled its location. The rest was a matter of guiding the kelpie on the right vector. This was almost two hours after leaving behind the molten glow of the trough and the cool, misty rains that drenched them amid blasts of thunder and lightening. They eventually entered a fogged region and later emerged from it to discover themselves above the cloud cover and in the full light of Beta.

At the apex, a concave wave-top stretched to either side for eternity, reflecting the stars, they arrived at the buoy and kept pace with it to await the others.

Spire whale pods roamed up and over the bulge, majestic and silent, sometimes brooding and echoing with the cries of kelpies and abbies, or the deep song of young whales.

The others, the four that remained, arrived on Luchadora some time later. None of them had much to say: some embraces, some tears. He'd remember forever the moment he and Boski met eyes. She'd lost an arm, and still sat high in the saddle. He waiting for her condemnation, but instead she pulled him into a one-armed embrace that suffocated him for a moment, kelpies whining side-by-side.

"We queried the transfer orbital, to see if someone could drop to the buoy," Amr explained. Cancer had grown quiet and didn't utter a word to him, her mother, or the others.

They could keep pace with the buoy, hoping someone got the message and intended to come for them, or they could travel out over the trailing bulges. Khalid suggested they disable the buoy and tow it behind them, to draw attention via whatever orbital monitoring paid attention to the platform.

"No," Pristina said. Amr had no idea how she knew the kelpie, Luchadora, would find it, but she let it lead them to a passing spire city and a group of hollow shells where they rode out the hours and bulges that followed and saw them again to low tide.

They took the buoy with them.

The slick vessel, *Steerpike's Folly*, hovered near the spire city in low tide. Under the bright glow of Alpha, they trudged from the pod and its surrounding detritus, to meet the ship and crew. The captain was an Anglo named Ginn, a big, jovial man who had a passing acquaintance with Fantomas.

"Your captain?" he asked from the Folly's ramp as they neared.

Pristina shook her head and the man gave a curt nod, face stricken.

"You'll want to know, one other of your crew survived. Your foreman, in fact."

"What?"

"One of the other ships set down near the spire city he walked from. Picked up tags left on several of the spires. Apparently there were others but they all fell victim to merfolk."

Amr wanted to say something, but Boski put her hand on his arm.

"And the others, on *Prayers to Mecca*?"

The captain said he'd check and sent word to his bridge.

"In the mean time—"

Out of nowhere, the fist lobbed him in the side of the face and Amr fell sprawling, half in the salty water, half on the metal ramp. He tasted copper. Cancer straddled him and landed three more blows to his face before anyone reacted. Two more glancing strikes, and his ship's mum had slicks from the Folly pull her off.

"Slicks, lay her out on the deck, one of you per wrist and ankle," Pristina ordered. The men faltered, unsure expressions tilted in their captain's direction.

"You'll treat Lady Patton-Guerrero as if she were our very own ship's mum," Ginn said, but Amr could tell he felt troubled by the odd order she'd given.

They clambered up into the neon-bright bay, past the reservoir, and onto the metal deck beyond. Already Cancer lay sprawled on the deck, held by a slick at each appendage. Pristina barked orders for more slicks to hold her shoulders *so she doesn't unsocket them*, she said. Cancer caught sight of Amr and started screaming.

"I hate you. I hate you!" spittle flew, her face scrunched.

"What else?" Pristina asked.

The screaming went on for a long time, mounting when Pristina knelt down and roughly cut the long locks from her daughter's head, then called for a trimmer. The girl cussed and cursed them, and when the trimmer that arrived a few minutes later hummed against her head, she cried. Cancer blubbered and shrieked, thrashing to get free.   Pristina had Khalid hold her head still, trimming the hair from all but the back of it, Amr suspected. The ship's mum stood.

"Now, and finally, you are a slick," she said to her daughter. Tears flowed from her eyes and her voice sounded thick. "Let her work the rest of it out, then let her up," she said to Boski and the other slicks holding her down. She strode away, Ginn taking her arm with a glance back at Cancer.

"I'm the last, you bitch. I'm the last slick. The last, you hear me? I'm going to destroy you all," Cancer continued on in this fashion for longer than Amr would care to remember.

By the end, he found himself crying too, and he didn't care. One of the *Folly*'s slicks patted his back, approval offered for the grief. Amr didn't care either way.

Through the course of it he overheard: none of the slicks sent to *Prayers to Mecca* ever made it. They were all lost. Pristina and Ginn must have returned to check on Cancer. The captain speculated that another swarm of ghost sharks may have reached the other group.

Amr wiped at the tears, but deep inside he felt cold. *I'm the last slick* she screamed, over and again. Cancer: her name appropriate. She would bring it all to an end.

She would be the last slick.

Here ends the study of slick life and labor called On the Demise of Captain Fantomas Patton-Guerrero and Loss of La Amenaza Elegente, *as documented and compiled by Dar al-Salam associate professor Pristina Patton-Guerrero.*

Hereafter follows the tale of Cancer Patton-Guerrero, the settlement she founded, and her eventual disappearance.

Thereafter, concluding the Guerrero story, is the tale of when La Amenaza Elegente's *remaining crew returned to the deep, and why.*

About the author

Brandon H. Bell is a writer of weird fiction and editor of the print magazine *Fantastique Unfettered*. His work has appeared in publications from M-Brane Press & Hadley Rille, as well as markets such as the *LovecraftEzine, Nossa Morte, and Everyday Weirdness*. He is an advocate for sensible copyright and Creative Commons licensing, a husband, a father, a Rissho Kosei-kai Buddhist, a member of The Outer Alliance, supporting his GLBTQ counterparts in the genre community, and, by day, he works in information systems security. Find out more through his blog, or search for Brandon H. Bell on Amazon, Barnes & Nobles, and elsewhere to find other print publications featuring his work.

Online at http://nithska.blogspot.com
Twitter: @nithska and
http://www.fantastique-unfettered.com

www.ingramcontent.com/pod-product-compliance
Lightning Source LLC
Chambersburg PA
CBHW020243180626
46810CB00006B/2342